FOLLOW UPTOWN BOOKS ON INSTAGRAM

http://www.instagram.com/uptownbooks_publishing

If you enjoyed this title by Shontaiye, check out **Messiah Raye**, also under Uptown Books.

https://www.amazon.com/-/e/B01L3N8SWE

Questions/Comments/Add to Mailing List

Email us at

uptownbookspublication@yahoo.com

If you enjoy reading, please leave a review.

Cash Rules Everything Around Me

SHONTAIYE

Uptown Books
1147 S. Salisbury Blvd
Suite 8-191
Salisbury, MD, 21801

This is a work of fiction. All of the characters, organizations, and events portrayed in this novel are either products of the author's imagination or are used fictitiously.

Cash Rules Everything Around Me. Copyright © 2018 Uptown Books. All rights reserved. No part of this book may be used or reproduced in any manner whatsoever without written permission except in the case of brief quotations embodied in critical articles or reviews.

ACKNOWLEDGEMENTS

I would like to thank everyone that has actually read my book. My childhood dream was to tell stories. I feel honored when what I've written, is actually read. I'll keep writing as long as you keep reading. Thank you.

INTRODUCTION TO THE END

"You got that?" I heard my roommate ask a fellow inmate icily as she stood over top of her. My roommate Dana was a butch; a girl who spoke, acted, and presented herself as a male.

"My order was messed up," the girl said, referring to her commissary; goods the jail let inmates order and pay for. She was scared. I noticed she was trembling.

"They didn't give me everything I had requested," she lied timidly. She looked scared and she had every reason to be. Dana was doing life in the Federal Penitentiary we were housed at, and she didn't play any games went it came to business. She took it very seriously. She was the block's loan shark. She leant out things with interest and you would either pay her back with more stuff or have someone deposit money on her books. She gave people reasonable time to pay up and if you didn't, she would just take it out your ass.

"You're lying. Several people have said you owed them too, and they've gotten their shit … so where's mine?" she asked, not really expecting an answer.

"I guess I'll just get my shit whenever you feel like giving it to me, right?" Dana continued sarcastically.

She stared down at the petite white girl I knew as Mandy, with menacing eyes. Mandy didn't respond. She didn't know what to say since Dana was dead on. I guess the silence didn't go over well with Dana. Before Mandy could get another word out, Dana punched her in the face so hard, she fell out of her chair and crumpled to concrete floor.

Dana knelt down and whispered to her, "Now you got to pay me triple … Late fees," she said menacingly, before walking off and heading back into the 6'8 cell we shared. I shook my head but said nothing. The girl was lucky. It could have been worse for her, and if she knew what was good for her, she would just pay up like Dana requested. The next beat-down she received would probably be less pleasant.

Walking off, I retreated back in my cell and sat down at the small desk. I rubbed my temples and looked at the picture of my smiling family stuck to the wall with toothpaste. We didn't have tape, and thumbtacks weren't allowed, nor would they go through the concrete walls, so we improvised.

I closed my eyes and thought back to the life I had. I used to complain about everything so much. Without a doubt, I took it for granted. I missed my family, my home, my job, and my car. I had been so greedy. I should have stopped while I was ahead, but

I didn't. I should have walked away from a lot of people, but I didn't. I made bad choices and now I'm paying the price and learning the hard way. I was once told that jealousy is the cousin of greed: it was only a matter of time that the two met up in my life. I'm Nijah, and this is my story.

ONE

Two Years Ago

NEVER IN A million years would I had ever thought I would be the target of blackmail. Yet, here I was sitting by the phone shaking like a leaf: waiting to be told, what I was, and wasn't going to do. I was somebody's bitch.

To say I was scared would be an understatement. My mama had always told me greed catches up with you, and she was right. I had enough problems to deal with; as if I needed another one.

I shifted around nervously while I waited for the caller to call back. The plush leather couch I sat on felt sticky against my sweaty skin. I tapped my bare foot nervously against the floor. I wasn't sure what my next move would be, but for now, the only option I had was to comply with the callers' demands.

The phone rang. It was abrupt and harsh, causing me to jump. I took a deep breath and swiped the answer button on my iPhone. The normally comfortable air-conditioned room, felt hotter than normal. Small beads of sweat had formed on my nose, but I didn't bother to wipe them off; I was focused on the message of the anonymous caller.

"I want half a mill," the person coldly and abruptly stated to me on the other line. The voice was deep and exaggerated. I could tell they were using something to distort the sound. I couldn't even tell if it was male or female

"I know what you do, I know what you've made, and I want half." The voice paused. "I'll text you the account information. You have a week. No funny shit, or I'll expose you and your sister to the IRS."

The abrupt absence of sound alerted me that the call had been disconnected, so I slowly placed the phone back down beside me. I stared down at the carpeted floor as the feeling of stress and grief washed over me. Dread sat in the pit of my stomach while thoughts of what I would do flooded my mind. I didn't have that type of money to hand over to anyone. Certainly, I had made it many times over during several years, however, I had been a reckless spender and recently called myself investing some of the dirty money I had made in multiple ventures.

I only had about $200,000 in cash, *but* I owned my house, and I also had a handful of rental properties throughout the city. Unfortunately, however, many of the rental properties required repair work that constantly required capital to go out. I also had just started buying equipment for a nail bar I was opening. I had assets but not $500,000 in cold, hard cash like the caller wanted.

The scheme I was involved in was supposed to be over. I had done it for a couple of years just to put me where I needed to be. At the time I had a job, but I needed a lump sum of money to secure me and my daughter's future.

I wondered who would do something like this to me? I would figure it out sooner or later, but for now I had to find a way to make a move to come up with some money. I had always been a go-getter, and nothing had changed. The only thing that was different, was that the stakes were higher.

<><><>

Briana looked at me from across her kitchen table with tear stained cheeks. The puffy bags around her eyes indicated that she had likely been crying. Stress shown all over her pretty, brown face.

"What are we going to do Nijah?" she asked me wearily. "I don't have $250,000." She rose up from the table and retrieved a gold and black bottle of Chardonnay off the granite counter, refilling her glass for the second time in five minutes.

I sighed deeply. My head had begun throbbing earlier as the stress of the events weighed heavily on my mind. I didn't have the answer. For some reason, she always expected me to.

Massaging my temples with my left hand, I responded in a low voice without looking at her, "I don't know Briana."

Finally making eye contact I said, "I'm going to sleep on everything and maybe we can come up with something tomorrow. We gotta do something though. If we sit around and do nothing, we're screwed. Onney will most definitely lose her job, and we'll end up owing the IRS millions."

I shuddered at the mere mention of the Internal Revenue Service. They had the power to touch the untouchables. We were no match for them, and truth be told, I was terrified.

"Most importantly, we'd definitely do jail time. We can't risk it. We're gonna have to pay them off. *How* we'll do that is the question? I don't want to even take a chance by messing with the fake taxes since that's what's got us jammed up in the first place. This is crazy," I said, as a rubbed at my temple again in frustration.

"Have you even told Onney yet?" she asked through glassy eyes.

I rolled my eyes since Briana already knew the answer to the question she was asking.

"Of course not," I finally responded impatiently. Briana was beginning to tick me off. I was the one getting the calls, and now it was up to me to figure out how to get us out of the mess by coming up with a plan, *and* I also had to be the one to tell Onney. As usual, all the problems would fall on me while Briana kicked back and waited for me to figure everything out. I had enough problems already. I watched as she took another gulp out of her wine glass. I guess she would worry, wait, and drink.

"She didn't want to get involved from the beginning, but we begged her," I continued. "Now this happens. For now, I'm going to hold off on telling her anything. At least until I come up with a plan. She'll flip when she hears what's going on. On top of that, I don't trust Onney no further that I can spit. She'll likely fold under pressure. I want to figure out our next move, and then let her know what's up."

I pushed my long black hair behind my ears and exhaled again deeply. I was still a little rattled from earlier. After pondering over that dreaded call, I finally decided to call it an early day and make my way back home. I hugged my sister and left quietly, except for the sound of my Gucci Sofia, high heeled booties tapping against Briana's shiny, hard wood floors.

After safely climbing into the driver seat of my new model, black Mustang GT, I grabbed my iPhone from my glove compartment and called my daughter's father Rashid. He answered after the sixth ring.

"Damn, what the hell took you so long to answer the phone? Let me talk to Layla please," I grumbled.

I had a serious attitude and was taking it out on him just because. I hadn't even bothered to say hello. I hated when Rashid acted like he didn't see the phone ringing, when he knew full well he was probably right on it texting. He always had his phone.

"Hi to you too Nijah," Rashid replied sarcastically. I didn't have to see the smirk on his face, but I definitely heard it. "My phone was in the other room," he explained. "Hold on, here she goes," he said, before passing the phone to our daughter.

After a bit of shuffling, I finally heard my daughters' syrupy voice in combination with all the background noise.

"Hi mommy," my daughter Layla greeted me cheerfully.

"Hey baby, whatchu doing?" I asked, automatically changing the tone of my voice. That quick, I had switched to Mommy mode. Layla was my heart and soul, the reason why I opened my eyes and breathed every morning.

"Playing with my cousins. My daddy took us to Coco's Fun House and we got in the bouncy," she revealed excitedly.

Coco's was a well-known local business. It was basically a giant play room for kids, with oversized, inflatable bounce houses they could jump on until they tired themselves out. They had some that resembled castles, dragons, and even characters like Thomas the Train.

"Oh, wow honey. Sounds like you're having a ball. I'm jealous. Well you keep having fun, and mommy will come pick you up tomorrow. Tell Daddy to have you ready around twelve, okay. Love you babe, mwah!" I said, making kissing sounds into the phone.

"Ok mommy. Love you too," she replied quickly and then proceeded with an exaggerated smooch through the phone.

I laughed and hung up the phone with the intention of calling back later to let Rashid know that I would be picking Layla up at noon tomorrow. I smiled again to myself at Layla's phone kiss. I loved her so much. She was the reason behind my madness, the reason why I woke, breathed, and ultimately schemed.

<><><>

Four years ago, when Layla was four, she became suddenly ill. What began as a suspected cold, grew worse, and was eventually diagnosed as a severe case of Pneumonia. She spent four weeks in the hospital and went from a chubby, forty pound four-year-old, to a thirty-pound child who would barely eat. It was devastating for me since I couldn't do anything for her pain or be there for her like I wanted to. Layla wanted her mommy around the clock, but mommy had to bring in some sort of income to make sure we still had a place to live.

My job was more than understanding, but I still didn't have enough paid time off to take an extended leave from work to be with Layla like I wanted. Rashid had just got out of jail and would sit with her half the day, however, he worked second shift and was on parole, so he too eventually had to go to work. I ended up cutting my hours to be there with her the remainder of the day when he left, as well as overnight.

In that short month, my finances took a negative blow. Since I was cutting my hours to be at the hospital, my income plummeted. On top of that, my insurance wasn't covering the entire cost of Layla's hospitalization. Just that quickly, I was thrust into debt and struggling to make ends meet. Rashid helped as much as he could, but it still wasn't enough. Luckily tax season had just approached, enabling me to use my returns to catch up on most of my bills.

When tax time did finally come, an idea ended up hitting me. Every year I watched people who sat on their behinds all year filing fake returns. These same people wound up getting back several thousand dollars for absolutely nothing. The majority of the time the IRS never caught them, even though they filed the dummy returns every year. Why couldn't I do that, just on a different level? I even had the perfect type of person to file the dummy returns for: prisoners. My scheming mind had a plan that would put me and Layla, right where we needed to be.

The typical inmate never filed tax returns since he or she was incarcerated. My plan was to file dozens of fake returns and rake in thousands off each one. The first year I filed twenty fake returns and ended up with around $50,000 in cash from Uncle Sam. That's when I decided that it would be, *go big or go home*. The second year I filed one hundred dummy returns with the help of my sister Briana. The third and fourth year, two hundred. The last two years, Briana and I were bringing in almost a quarter million dollars apiece.

We only targeted inmates who had life sentences and would never see daylight again. The way we obtained their information was by sending letters with fraudulent contact information which said that we were an organization that helped inmates get new trials and would help get their convictions overturned. We asked for prison id number, case details, and ultimately, personal information such as date of birth, and social security numbers. Ninety-nine percent of these inmates willingly gave this information, with hopes that one day they would be free.

Our older sister Onney works at one of the state prisons in upstate Pennsylvania. Although pretty, my sister had always been a little heavyset and a bit of a tomboy, so it was fitting for her to take a job as a correctional officer. As a Lieutenant she was able to access sensitive information on inmates in Pennsylvania who have life in prison. With her connection, we had a list of "lifers," male and female, in all of Pennsylvania as well as the surrounding states. For that information we gave her 10% of what we brought in every tax season. Onney usually walked away with about $50,000 while Briana and I took home around $250,000.

The money literally changed my life. I was able to put Layla in private school, purchase stocks and bonds, buy several properties, take trips all over the world, and surround myself with items I could only have dreamed of. It was a risky situation that we knew we couldn't continue forever. Even though I had burnt through a lot of money, I had wised up the past year and had been investing my money, so I would have something to build on, and be secure in the future. Briana didn't have children and blew money like it was nothing. I'm sure she wasn't broke, but I bet that she didn't have much to show from four years of scheming.

Onney on the other hand, I wasn't so sure about. She lived three hours away, so we rarely saw much of her. She had been hesitant to go along with the plan initially, trying as best she could to minimize her involvement. It was actually Briana's idea to bring her in on everything

Before Onney's involvement I had been obtaining prisoner information online through public court records. Onney and I had never really been close, so I knew if anything ever happened, she would probably turn on us at the speed of lightning. One thing about me is that I had morals, so if shit ever hit the fan, my lips were sealed. However, I couldn't speak for anyone but myself.

I didn't sleep well that night with thoughts of possible prison time running through my mind. I didn't want my daughter to end up in the foster care system like I did. I didn't have any family besides my sisters, so my daughter would basically have no one if I got drug down behind this tax fraud shit. She had her dad part-time, but to me he was unreliable since he was usually in and out of jail for drugs. I had to think long and hard about my next move, so I could get out of the shit's creek I had fell in.

TWO

BOOM! BOOM!

The sound of banging at my door woke me abruptly out of my sleep. "What in the hell?" I asked no one in particular.

Still slightly disoriented, I jumped out of my warm bed and stumbled down the carpeted but still cold hallway, to see who was at my door. After peering through the peephole, I saw that it was a smiling Rashid and Layla.

"What the hell is wrong with you?" I asked, clearly annoyed, while opening the door. "Why would you bang on the door like that? You scared me." I figured it was still early and I definitely wasn't a morning person. It shown on my face.

I wiped a small piece of crust out of my eye, and let the two of them in. Layla immediately dropped her bag, gave me a hug and kiss, then proceeded to her room to play with her volcano pile of toys. At her age, she was happily self-absorbed.

"It's two o clock and I just came by to check on you since Layla said you would be by to pick her up at 12," Rashid stated, quickly peering around the house and then turning his gaze to me.

Rashid's intense stare burned a hole through me, causing me to feel a little uncomfortable. Once I realized I jumped out of the bed with nothing on but my bra and thong, I understood what his eye problem was all about.

At five foot four, I was extremely thick. I wasn't the ideal video vixen with the big butt and unrealistic small waist; I instead, was built like a brick house, thick all over and very bottom heavy. I wasn't fat though. I was one of those types that people assumed came from a family of voluptuous women. Hands down, my figure drew its fair share of stares. I was a black man's dream come true, with a pretty, chocolate face to match.

"I overslept," I said, before running my fingers through my disheveled hair, trying my best to make myself look presentable.

"And stop looking at me like that," I demanded. "Let me go put on something really quick."

I rolled my eyes and walked off to the back of my house to put on some clothes. My round chocolate butt jiggled as I made my way to do that. Rashid came right behind me.

"You don't gotta change. I'm not worried about

you. We need to talk anyway," Rashid said, as he followed me into my room.

"Talk about what?" I snapped, still a little sleepy and irritated from being woken up. "Layla?" I asked sarcastically.

Ever since Rashid and I had broken up six years ago, he always wanted to "talk." I had no desire to entertain him unless it was about our daughter. One minute he pretended he was cool living the single life, then the next minute he wanted a family with us. To hell with all that. I had no desire to be with Rashid on that level anymore. Throughout the three years we were together, he did nothing but lie and cheat. During the time we were together he became arrogant, like I was supposed to put up with his crap. It also didn't help that somewhere along the line he formed a habit of being in and out of jail.

"Damn Nijah. I changed. I'm through with all the bull," he said, referring to his notorious cheating ways and multiple stints in jail. "Besides, Layla could use her dad around the house, and you could use the help. We could make it work, just on a mature level this time," Rashid suggested, sounding sincere.

I took a deep breath and finally responded arrogantly. I wasn't really trying to. "Rashid honey … I'm good. I can handle things on my own, and I have my own money. I don't have time to go backwards."

"What you seeing somebody or something?" he asked with attitude. He frowned his face up jealously.

"No, it's not that. I'm just focused, and I don't

have time to deal with the negativity you bring. I'm on a whole different chapter in my life … and besides I know my worth."

Rashid just peered at me for ten seconds. I guess let what I had said register.

Rashid shot me a dirty look. "Oh, it's like that?" he asked with disappointment.

"Yeah. It is," I replied coolly.

"Aight cool. Well I guess I'll just say bye to my daughter then."

Rashid walked out of the room to go say bye to Layla and about thirty seconds later, I heard the door close. I sighed. I was glad he left. Rashid was such a pain. I decided to get myself together so I could make an early dinner for Layla.

***

Two hours later I had finished making our Sunday dinner of: smothered chicken wings, mashed potatoes, and green beans with tomatoes. I definitely put it down on Soul-food Sundays before it was time to be back to work on Monday.

Despite my illegal activities and to maintain some level of normalcy, I still worked forty hours a week as a Claims Representative for the health care giant Aetna. I had come along ways from being the poor little black Nijah who was in and out of foster homes. I had never known my father, and my mother had been killed in a home invasion when I was ten. Briana was nine and Onney was fourteen when our lives were turned upside down by the tragic event. The rumor was, she was killed in a crack house that was known for having a number of ruthless, heavy weight drug-dealers around. Whoever robbed the spot wasn't taking any chances and leaving witnesses.

Even though my mom was a crack-head, she had been a functioning addict. She worked in housekeeping at a hotel, and for the most part we remained clean and fed. For some reason my mother just found comfort from getting high. She had struggled with depression for as long as I could remember, and after my grandmother passed away, she kind of zoned out and things took a turn for the worst. She stopped functioning. I guess the loss, along with depression and being a single mother, took its toll on her.

My mom had a sister, but she too was pre-occupied with getting high to come help raise her orphaned nieces. She wasn't even close to being considered a functioning addict. She was one of those bad teeth, prostituting drug addicts. Ultimately, we wound up being in and out of foster homes until we turned 18. Onney ended up being separated from us since it was easier to place younger children. No one really wanted to be bothered with foul-mouthed, emotional and problematic teenagers.

Luckily for me and Briana, we had a good caseworker who worked hard at keeping us together. We never stayed gone from one another long, since our worker Ms. Evans, always fought tooth and nail to get us both placed in the same home. However, we often times went months without speaking to Onney, who over time, turned into someone we barely knew. Even to this day she is very isolated and secretive. It took us months to learn she had moved to Northern Pennsylvania to take a job as a corrections officer. Even when she got married to another C.O, it was unknown to us and discovered months later through a general conversation.

After Layla went to bed I decided to relax and reflect back on yesterday's events. I poured a glass of my favorite red wine and ran myself a hot bath in the oversized tub that drew me to buy the home in the first place.

I looked around my private master bath and realized how much I had. Clearly, I hadn't earned it *all*, but something inside of my mind forced me to believe that I was entitled to it. I deserved the small, but beautiful townhome in the upscale development that I lived in. I deserved to be able to take trips to Aruba to lie on a beautiful beach with green water. Yes, *green* water, not blue.

I grew up in foster homes. I went to home after home where I wasn't wanted. When I turned eighteen I was on my own and essentially homeless, living in a shelter until I was able to get a job that allowed me to afford a small room in a rooming house. That same room I shared with Briana when she became of age, until we were finally able to get an apartment. I worked my ass off for years and finally got a break when I graduated from community college and got a job with Aetna. Didn't I deserve all that I had, no matter how I obtained it? Needless to say, no one could tell me otherwise.

THREE

IT WAS THE following Monday, so I dropped Layla off at her private school bright and early at 8:15. I had taken the day off, so I could make my way around and verify repairs were being made on several of my properties. After speaking with my contractor and visually verifying repairs, I was pleased.

It was 2:15 in the afternoon when I sat down in the small booth at Chili's downtown. All four of my properties were in North Philly, so it was convenient to have lunch there. I checked the time on my rose gold Michael Kors watch; Briana was running late as usual, so I decided to order some spinach dip to quiet the hunger pangs in my stomach.

I had eaten all of my appetizer and was nibbling on dry nachos when Briana showed up. It was 3 pm and she was almost an hour late. Luckily for her, I was a laid-back person and I didn't sweat the small stuff.

"Wassup chick, what took you so long?" I asked, before taking a sip of water.

"Girl you know traffic in Philly is terrible. Plus, I had to drop off my homeboy." She looked cute with a royal blue pant suit on and oversized gold accessories. A messy bun complimented her funky look.

"Homeboy? I haven't heard anything about this so-called homeboy," I said, before pausing. I was extremely curious, but I remained quiet. Briana loved to talk, and showing interest but keeping quiet, was my way of silently encouraging her to spill. This way I could avoid asking and appearing nosey.

"You don't remember Eric? We met him at the casino. Tall, dark-skinned, with the tats on his neck?" she said, describing him so I could remember.

"Oh yeah, the hood looking dude. He was cute though," I said remembering the night.

"Yeah, that's my boo," Briana giggled, while fumbling around in her purse until she found her mirror.

I rolled my eyes internally. Everybody was her boo. I'll admit, we both had the worst taste in men. We liked them hood and ninety percent of the time, they weren't worth a darn. Only problem was, Briana could be naïve, and most guys took advantage of her because of it. The crazy part was Briana was a very pretty girl. Although she had an athletic build, it complimented her petite frame. She was brown skinned with golden highlights that made her light brown eyes glow. She reminded me a lot of Zoe Saldana.

Briana's main issue was she could be an airhead at times. Her lack of conversation, as well as her lack of motivation, didn't get her far with guys of quality. Nevertheless, that was my baby sister and I'd knock a chick's head off for her.

"Well that's wassup. I gotta meet him one day soon," I said, lying. I had no interest whatsoever of meeting any of her so called "homeboys."

"I'm surprised you haven't yet. We be together most of the time," she said, while staring into her compact mirror and fixing her strip eyelashes.

"Oh yeah?" I laughed. "That's why you be MIA, not answering the phone?"

"Whatever Trick. Let's talk about you and Rashid." She took one more look at herself, closed the mirror, and stuffed it back in her purse. Briana was very self-absorbed.

"Definitely nothing to talk about there. I'm focused and I ain't worried about no nigga if his name isn't *Money*. Besides at this point, we have bigger fish to fry and don't have time to be fooling with niggas." If I remembered correctly, we were both being blackmailed.

As soon as I made the comment Briana became irritated. She looked down and pretended to observe her polished blue nails.

"Whatever. So wassup?" she asked jokingly,

doing her best to conceal her light attitude.

Briana didn't like people judging her, especially me. She always thought I was trying to tell her she was messing up. That wasn't exactly the case, but at the moment, the last thing that should be on her mind was a broke, scheming nigga.

I decided to change the subject to keep the peace. Lord knows, I didn't feel like cursing her out today.

"I called you to meet me because I got another phone call this morning," I said seriously, getting down to business. We have until tomorrow to wire this money. They want a half million but that's definitely not happening. I figure we could stall them by giving them $50G's. I figure we would split it." It was more of a statement than a question.

I paused for Briana to respond. I was praying she had half of the fifty thousand. To many, it would seem like small change compared to what we had made, however, like typical folk who weren't used to having anything, we ran through it like the speed of lightning.

"Aight, looks like we have no choice right," she responded casually.

Briana was one of those people who hid their emotions very well. You would never be able to tell she was going through something until she snapped. Here we were being extorted and she comes in giggling about her new boyfriend. I on the other hand was the exact opposite. I engaged Briana in conversation to keep the peace. She was one of those people you had to accept for who they were and deal with on their terms, otherwise you'd always find yourself arguing and at odds. Being as though she was one of the very few family members I had, I often found myself biting my tongue and letting a lot of things go unsaid. It was pretty much how it had always been.

"You're right. We really don't have a choice, however, what I'm worried about is, what if we pay them, and they don't stop. Then this mess will never end." I stared off, looking at nothing in particular.

Briana shifted around in the worn red booth. "I guess we'll just figure that out when the time comes. We can't really cry over spilt milk; we just gotta do our best to clean it up. It's messed up, but we'll get through it. I'll have my money in the morning though."

She glanced down at her vibrating phone on the table. I noticed her frequent peeks at her phone, so I figured I would wrap up our conversation.

"I'm gonna let you get back to ya boo. Plus, it's after four, so I gotta make my way back to Willow Grove to pick up Layla from school."

I dropped an eight-dollar tip on the table and rose up to give Briana a kiss on the cheek. We never received affection from adults as children, since most foster parents didn't like to form bonds and attachment to the children they were caring for. So, we made up for it by giving it to one another.

"Aight boo, I'll meet up with you tomorrow then."

<><><>

The drive to pick up Layla was longer than expected. There had been a fender bender and it was causing delays. I sucked my teeth and cursed in frustration. I had no choice but to grin and bear it. As I crawled through the mid-day traffic, I thought about wiring the money in the morning. *What if things went wrong? What if it wasn't enough in the end? Even if we paid them the full amount, what if they still continued to black mail us?*

No matter what, we were going to lose. *How bad we would lose*, was the question. At lunch, Briana had insisted we tell Onney what was going on. She thought she may have some money to contribute to the payoff.

Of course, she introduced the idea, but it wound up being me who would deliver the unwelcome news. At the rate things were going, it didn't really even matter how she took it. No matter how you look at things, what we had been doing was illegal.

After pondering for hours, the only thing I had determined was we would need to file more phony returns to get the money the crook was looking for. I didn't have that type of money, nor was I giving up all that I had. The biggest problem we faced was that it was the end of March, and tax season was about to end. How the hell would we file over two hundred returns in two weeks? It was crunch time, and I prayed Briana and Onney were prepared.

I made it to Layla's school at 5:37. The after-school program she was in, let out at 5:30. I hated being late to pick up my angel. She saw me as soon as I pulled up. She was standing near the glass double doors at the entrance of the school. I waved to the teacher to confirm I was there for her.

Shortly after, Layla walked out with her round eyes beaming and her ponytails wagging. She skipped to the car carrying her Hello Kitty backpack. Her hair was slightly disheveled, and she looked like the typical messy nine-year-old with lunch stains on her uniform shirt. Despite all of that, she made my heart melt.

"Hey doll face." I leaned over to give her a kiss as she got into the car.

"Hey mommy. Why are you late?" she asked, with curiosity displayed on her pretty brown face.

"I'm sorry doll. The traffic was bad. I had met Auntie Briana for lunch and loss track of time."

"Oh. I thought you had forgot me," she said seriously, while fastening her seatbelt.

"Of course, not silly, I would never forget you," I said.

"Well can you try to be on time tomorrow? A new Disney movie comes on tomorrow at six, and I need to have my homework done in time to see it. I missed the original premier, so I don't want to miss this showing."

I smiled and replied. "You got it. 5:30 sharp."

I shook my head. My daughter hardly had a care in the world. I made a vow that day that I would do everything necessary to ensure that it stayed that way.

After helping with homework and making dinner, I called Onney to let her know what was going on. Of course, she took it the way I expected her to take it.

"So, what happens now?" I heard her exhale a deep breath. She was whispering into the phone and sounded like she was moving around the house.

"Well, I'm going to deposit $50,000 into the account after they give me the number tomorrow. I'm going to see if I can give them the other $450,000 after I file these returns."

"Gosh Nijah. Do you even have enough names left on the list to even file that many returns? With this kind of crap going on, there's no way I would think about trying to get more names out of the prison database. Who could be doing this? I don't have any enemies and I didn't tell anyone about this, not even my husband." She was still whispering and shuffling around in the house.

"I don't know. Briana and I talked about this the other day, and we couldn't come up with an answer. You know my circle is small, and I definitely don't go around telling anyone my business."

"Yeah. Well, what about Briana. She always had a big mouth, even when we were kids."

Onney and Briana never really cared much for one another. They weren't close and wouldn't be in contact if it weren't for me. They were exact opposites, with Onney being work-orientated and quiet, and Briana outgoing and loud.

"True, but Briana knows the consequences behind our actions. She's not stupid."

Onney grew irritated at what she considered my naive attitude. "Bottom line is people are deceitful and someone who knows one of us, is blackmailing us."

I shifted the phone to my other palm since the one I was using had grown sweaty. I was beginning to get irritated with my older sister. She surely had a lot to say with no money to contribute. However, Onney was right about what she way saying; someone we knew was blackmailing us. One thing for sure, whoever it was would have hell to pay when I found out. I hung up the phone with her and promised to call back the following night.

After hanging up the phone with Onney, I realized that Rashid was right, and we did need to talk. I needed his help. Ever since I was a child I was one of those people that did what they had to do, whether I wanted to or not. This was one of those times. I didn't like showing people that I was vulnerable; however, I had to be a woman and go to Rashid to let him know that I didn't have it all together at this point. It was extremely important for Rashid to understand that I needed him to be there for Layla.

I wasn't going to tell him exactly what was going

on, but I was going to let him know that I needed him. It wasn't the easiest task to be faced with, especially since I had literally just cursed him out and kicked him out of my house the other day.

The truth was, Rashid wasn't all that bad. He was one of those types that made all the wrong decisions for the right reasons. We had been young when we got together, and he wasn't crap for a boyfriend, but he did really want his family to have. He had really tried to provide for us, even though he failed at it. Bottom line was, I needed to have a sit down with him.

<><><>

It was 12 am when Rashid knocked on the door. I sent him a text message earlier to see if he could come by, so we could talk. He had just gotten off his 3-11 shift at a meat manufacturing company, and still had on his work clothes when he showed up. I let him in, but this time I had on sweat pants and a tank top.

"You hungry?" I asked, greeting him with a half-smile.

"Yeah, I am," he replied quickly.

I walked off to the kitchen to warm up some of the leftover Baked Ziti I had made earlier. I made small talk with Rashid while he ate, and then finally decided to approach the dreaded conversation about the situation I was in. I pulled out a chair and sat adjacent to him at the counter height dining set. I wasn't sure where to begin.

"Rashid, I called you here tonight because I have some stuff going on my end. I can't really go into much details, but I need to know that if necessary, you will be there for Layla 100%." I stared at Rashid with a serious face.

He stopped eating and replied. "No doubt, but what's going on?"

"I can't really go into it too much, but I just need to know that you will be there for Layla and be a better father. I'm in a little bit of trouble and hopefully I can get out of it. The main thing for me is preparing for the worse but hoping for the best. My primary concern is Layla's well-being if something happens to me. Ultimately, you and I are all she has, and she depends on us."

"Whatever's going on with you, you don't have to tell me about it right now, but I will definitely be there for my daughter. And whenever you feel like talking about what's going on, or anything for that matter, I'm here. I know I haven't been the best, but those three years in prison changed me. I love yawl, even though you may not believe it. And I'ma prove that."

I smiled. I knew he would at least try. At that moment, I remembered what had attracted me to him in the first place.

Rashid stood six feet tall and was extremely handsome except for a long scar that went down the side of his light brown face. His eyes were round and had a darkness about them that hinted at a mysterious past. He had always been passionate and loving, even when he was doing wrong. I guess for those reasons, we fought hard and loved even harder. A girl like me could only take but so much though. He had been my everything and sharing him was something I just could not do under any circumstances. Over time, with too many wrongs, and not enough rights, the love I had turned to resentment and eventually faded. Well, that's what I forced myself to feel anyway.

I switched my focus to clearing the table. Ignoring Rashid and sticking to my cold attitude kept me from getting sucked into his web. This particular night, however, it was hard to do. I was going through something, making me very vulnerable, so of course my attitude reflected that.

Without making eye contact, I told Rashid he was more than welcome to sleep in the guest bedroom since I knew he was tired, and probably didn't feel like driving back to North Philly.

"Towels and wash cloths are in the linen closet near the bathroom and the washer and dryer is near the back door," I told him.

"Aight cool. And thanks, Nijah. I just want us to be friends. Honestly. I can't have things my way, so I'll take that rather that nothing at all. You a good chick for real and I messed up. I was young, but I do appreciate you letting me make it up by being a better father to my daughter. Hopefully one day you'll give *us* another chance."

I smiled at his seemingly sincere revelation and walked off to get some rest.

FOUR

THE NEXT MORNING, I was stressed to the max. Rashid had already dropped Layla off at school for me and went home to Germantown, a small, working class section within Philadelphia. I stayed home and sat in my bedroom to wait for "the" call. I hadn't yet told my blackmailer that I would not have a full half a million dollars. The money I would be depositing was in fact just that: a mere deposit. After staring at the phone for what seemed like an eternity, it finally rang. It was 11am and I had been waiting for almost two hours.

"Hello," I asked, speaking into the receiver.

"Do you have the money? If so I have the banking information for you and your sister to make the deposit." The voice was still distorted. I still had no idea who it was, nor could I tell if it was a male or female.

"I have $50,000," I blurted out. There was no need beating around the bush. This was serious, and I needed to know right then and there if they would take it or not.

"When will you have the rest?" the muffled voice asked.

"I need until May, and I also need your word that this will be done and over with. I will agree to your terms, but I need this to be over once we pay you."

"Done. But if you try to burn me, I'll ruin you. Understand?"

"I understand," I replied solemnly.

The caller gave me all the information I needed to make the deposit into the Bank of America account, so I headed over to Briana's house in the Mt. Airy section of Philadelphia.

When I pulled up to Briana's I noticed there was a blue, late model Chevy Monte Carlo parked in the driveway. It had gigantic chrome rims, and tinted windows. It was ghetto and screamed "Police, pull me over!" I figured it was her little jump off Eric, and I was pissed that she was more worried about being laid up, rather than answering her phone for something important. I had been calling her butt all morning.

I banged on the door for several minutes until she answered it. The sight of her angered me further, especially because she wasn't dressed, and she already knew she was supposed to go with me to make the deposit at the bank.

"Really?" I asked frowning, as she opened the door to let me in, which she seemed hesitant to do.

"My fault, I overslept, let me go get some clothes on." She proceeded to run back to the room in nothing but panties and bra set, showing off her small curves.

I couldn't believe she could oversleep on something as important as this. She was acting like this wasn't serious, and I made a mental note to check her when I got the opportunity.

"Hurry up," I yelled to her, as she ran off to get dressed.

Just as Briana was turning the corner to her bedroom, I heard another voice, which confirmed her priorities. Being nosey, I pretended I was going to the bathroom, but was nearly knocked over by Briana's thug boyfriend. In all actuality I bumped into him not paying attention, however, I was still agitated.

"My bad," I stammered, apologizing.

"Dang sis, you sleep?" he asked jokingly, displaying a set of perfect white teeth.

I laughed lightly and responded. "Naa. Long morning, and we need to get going. You must be Eric?" I asked.

Eric was actually extremely handsome in a rough and rugged kind of way. He rocked a set of fuzzy cornrows on his head and had a pleasant face with a strong jawline. Looking at him, I did in fact remember him from the casino that night. I could see why Briana was head over heels for him. He was the typical good-looking, bad boy that she always fell for.

"Yep, Yep. Nice to meet you," he replied.

"Well I'm Nijah," I said, forcing a smile on my face.

I was pretty sure he knew who I was, but figured it was polite to introduce myself. I really didn't care to make small talk but found it unavoidable since I had nearly knocked him over in the hallway. Just then, Briana turned the corner and saved me from the forced conversation.

"I see you two have met. You ready?" She looked at me as she smoothed her hair back and pulled an elastic band on it to secure it into a neat ponytail. Brushing her clothes off, she was now ready to go.

"Yeah, I'm ready," I replied.

The ride to the bank was quiet since I was still irritated with Briana. She didn't take anything seriously. On top of that she only had $20,000 and not the half of the money that we had originally agreed on. Because of her, I had to go out of the way to my own bank and take another $5,000 out of my personal savings account.

I honestly felt like I was going through this whole ordeal alone. I was focusing most of my time on dealing with the blackmailer, running behind Briana, and reasoning with Onney. On top of that I was working, being a single mom, and managing my properties. The nail bar had been put on hold for now, but I was beginning to get overwhelmed.

"Nijah watch out!" Briana yelled out, suddenly.

I slammed on the breaks so hard, our bodies jerked forward, and you could hear the tires screech. A group of teenagers had dashed across the road trying to catch the bus and had almost become road-kill. They continued across the street while giving me dirty looks. Briana was still perched forward in her seat, with her right hand clenching the door.

"Yo, what's wrong with you? You're spaced the hell out!" she yelled, with a bewildered look on her face.

I smacked my teeth in anger and irritation. "Nah, I'm stressed the hell out, and nobody is making it any better." I was about two seconds from slapping fire out her.

"Someone is extorting us for a quarter million dollars apiece and you're more worried about chasing behind a man, rather than dealing with the issue. Onney's no help and doesn't have a dime to put up. And you stay coming up short on everything but always got a new purse on ya arm. So, if anybody spaced out, it's you. You need a reality check, because clearly you're not in tune to what is happening."

Briana responded in a lowered tone, carefully choosing her words. "I am in tune. I just handle stress differently from you, but I'm going through something just like you. And Eric is not just any man I'm chasing. He's *my* man. That's your choice that you choose not to seek comfort from anyone."

"Seek comfort? Briana, you don't just go around telling people you're being blackmailed. That's something you, Onney and I should be dealing with together."

"That's not what I'm saying Nijah. I said *seek comfort*, not *confide*."

"Whatever. You need to be more active in coming up with a solution. It's always *me* trying to figure things out and hold everything together. It's *always* been like that ... You just make sure you're present when it's time to get the other $450,000. We have to file several hundred returns to get that kind of money, and we only have until May to do it."

Briana snapped her neck back and looked at me crazily. "May? You can't be serious. How are we going to file that many returns? We usually do that over 3 months."

"My point exactly," I said, hoping she now realized that we would basically be working non-stop and trying to pull off a miracle.

I made the turn on Broad Street and pulled the car into the Bank of America parking lot. Briana and I made our way into the bank and quickly made the deposit. Since it was still early, the line wasn't too long. Once the deposit was made, I sent out the text to confirm the transaction was done. Within two minutes I got a text that confirmed it was received.

Briana and I sat quietly in thought on the way home. As usual she was on her phone. I informed her that the tax filing would begin tomorrow, and that I needed her focused and present, so we could get the money we needed. It took weeks for tax refunds to come back, and we had two weeks at the most to file several hundred returns. We had to make sure all of them were error free, so there were no delays. We had our work cut out for us. Between my work schedule and managing repairs on my properties, I expected to pull some all-nighters.

<><><>

Later that night I thought about what Briana had said, and she did have a little bit of a point. I didn't have to go at the stress of my situation completely alone. Even though I had no man, I could silently find comfort within my friendships. I decided to call up my best girlfriend Asia. I had met her years back when I first started at Aetna and we had been very close friends since. With everything that had been going on, I hadn't spoken to her in like a week.

Asia had two kids and happened to be putting one to sleep when I called, so we only spoke briefly. However, we did make plans to meet up on Saturday for drinks. After speaking with her I called Onney. Surprisingly, she answered on the first ring.

"Hey Nijah," she said, sounding wide awake. It surprised me she answered on the first ring. Lately, I had been able to reach her with no problem. Before we were doing the tax scheme, it would sometimes take her days to return a phone call.

"Hey. You busy?" I asked.

"No. Why wassup?

"I just want to talk is all. It's a lot of pressure from this whole situation, and I'm starting to get frustrated. Just want to vent."

For a half an hour, I expressed my frustration with Briana, her lack of focus, and how I felt she wasn't taking the situation seriously. It was almost as if her mind was occupied on something else completely. Ever since she had met this guy Eric, it was as if her world became consumed around him, and it was proving harder and harder for me to get in contact with her. I wasn't used to that and it was somewhat disheartening since we had been really close.

After venting, Onney relieved some of her own frustrations she had pent up. She revealed that her and her husband had been having problems for years and had been even more at odds the past couple of months. He drank and had a gambling problem. For almost a year, she had been handling the bills solely on her income, while he gambled his away at the casino. She said that when he won big, he was generous and kind, but when he lost he was mean and drowned himself in alcohol. He still worked, but that too was in jeopardy because inmates were complaining about his aggression. More recently, he had begun questioning her finances after she leased a new car because her old one was giving her problems. I asked her why she put up with it, but her only reason was because she loved him, and they had been together for a long time. She admitted to that she couldn't let go. He had shown her a great deal of love and acceptance, something she didn't have growing up.

"Nijah, truthfully, I'm at my wits end. The mortgage is killing me, and the money I was getting with yawl was keeping me afloat. I don't know how much longer I can deal with this with Kevin.

"I don't know Onney... But if it makes you feel any better, I'm here if you need any help financially. I made some investments and I'm okay for now ... well, if everything plays out right with this situation anyway. My main concern is, what will you do over time? Clearly, we can't do this scheme anymore after we get this money to pay this person off. I mean ... if your mortgage is too much, and Kevin isn't helping, you may need to try to sell and downsize."

"I thought about that. It's other stuff too. It's just a lot." She sighed and paused.

Clearly, she had some bigger issues going on in that house. I made a vow to myself that day, that I would be a bigger part of Onney's life. Even when we were split up as kids, she went through that ordeal alone, unable to confide in her sisters. I wanted her to know that she always had me, and that if I could help, I would. It saddened me that she was being financially abused by her husband. Her perception of love was still distorted from childhood. The problem was, when people were so used to going without something they wanted and needed, they would sometimes settle for anything that felt close to it. It reminded me of my relationship with Briana. I pretty much accepted things for what they were because I wanted her love so badly. My small family was all I had.

I later ended the call with a newfound appreciation for my sister, as well as relationships in general. You never knew what a person was going through, and I was always so quick to judge.

FIVE

THE WEEK THAT followed was hectic just like I expected. My schedule at Aetna was 7a-3p, but I was still working until nearly seven in the evening because of my properties. The repairs to my two rooming houses were finally done, so I had been focused on getting the rooms rented. The remainder of my afternoon consisted of meeting with potential renters, getting keys made, and running back and forth to the bank to make deposits. Layla was staying at the daycare until seven, so I could handle business. By the time I got home, took a shower and made a quick pasta skillet dinner, I was beat.

Briana would meet me at 9 pm so we could work on filing returns for six hours. We were on a tight schedule and had been working 30 hours per week to meet our deadline. I would sleep when we were done and be back up at 5 am to get ready for work and drop Layla off at daycare. I had begun relying on caffeine to help me stay awake. Lately, Briana and I had become a bit distant. I was never the one to hate on anyone's happiness but lately she had been more of a sucker for love. She had been cheery despite the predicament that we were in. Although I found it odd, I never said anything to her ... that was, until she crossed the line.

It was Friday and I was waiting on Briana to show up to help me with returns. She was late, but I decided to let it ride. That is until she showed up to my home with her boyfriend. When I looked out the window and saw a man behind the wheel of her BMW, I saw red. Before Briana could open the door, I was on her behind like white on rice.

"I know damn well you didn't bring that nigga to my house?" I asked, looking at Briana like she'd lost her mind. I walked around her and looked out the window to confirm I was correct. Sure enough, it was Eric.

"He dropped me off, what are you tripping for?" she asked, looking confused.

"I don't care what lame you choose to deal with, but I don't want none of them broke, scheming niggas from North Philly at my house. You don't know him for-real Briana. Damn, you do some dumb shit." I said through clenched teeth, before walking off in aggravation.

Instead of walking away and letting me vent, Briana decided to follow behind me and argue.

"You know what Nijah, you always got ya nose stuck in the air like you better than everybody else. *You* don't know him, and that's my dude so I don't see what the problem is. And besides, you act like Rashid ghetto, drug-dealing ass isn't from North Philly."

Ignoring the statement about Rashid, I responded harshly. "I don't give a damn who he is. He isn't my man! He's your temporary nigga. Every time I turn around you got a new nigga. I don't want none of them around me, *or* around the place that I plan to permanently rest my head with my daughter. Hood niggas like that pick air-head, idiot chicks like you to *use*, and they see you coming from a mile away. As you can see he left his punk ass Monte Carlo in North Philly and is pushing your BMW instead. Niggas like that are leeches, and I could see it from the start, way back when we were at the casino. That's why I turned my head when the nigga was giving *me* the eye."

As soon as those words came out, I regretted saying it. I had a major problem with the way I communicated sometimes. However, by the time I realized what I said was wrong, it was too late.

Not to be conceited but I regularly received attention, especially from hood guys like Eric. I sure wasn't Beyoncé, but I was still certainly easy on the eyes. Unlike Briana, I was thick from top to bottom.

Thighs, hips, everything curvy and swollen. When Briana's boyfriend and his friends walked by us the night at the casino, they of course did a double take. We were both fly that night, but the whole time, her lame boyfriend Eric, was eyeing me like a piece of meat. Of course, I'm about Benjamin's, so I had no time to converse. Briana, of course took the bait, and that's why she was sitting there with the pissed face, mad because I was stating facts.

"You know what bitch, fuck you," she spat harshly. "You can do this crap by yourself. I'ma call my man to pick me up, while you sit ya lonely, miserable ass in here by yaself. Maybe Rashid will come over and make you happy by fuckin ya sad raggedy ass."

I laughed out loud, but I was certainly angry at the comment. "Yeah, I don't have to beg niggas to screw me. As a matter of fact, I could probably have ya man eating out the palm of my hand or eating from *anywhere* for that matter. Trust me."

Before I could say anything else, Briana hauled off and punched me upside my head and then proceeded to grab a handful of my $400 weave. My head instantly went down with my weave and I knew now for certain that my sister, was in fact crazy.

Briana landed a couple hard blows to my back while I used my body weight to keep from tumbling over the couch, since we were still in the living room. She had my long hair pulled down, wrapped around her hand in a death grip. Once I was able to regain my balance and had one foot planted firmly, I swung hard and punched her in the side. I didn't want to hurt her, but I wanted her to get off me. The blow did exactly what I hoped it would do, make her lose her breath and let go of my hair. When she let go, I rushed her, slammed her against the door and grabbed her collar.

"What the hell is wrong with you? I'll beat your ass in here!" I yelled, as I violently shook her against the hard, cherrywood door.

"All jokes aside, call ya nigga so you can get the hell out my house! You got me chopped — disrespecting me in my own home!"

Spittle flew from my mouth as I released her with a shove and walked off enraged. I couldn't believe she would attack me over a guy. I knew Briana was feeling dude, but for her to go against me, it had to be serious. We were too close for that. This stupid ass argument had gotten out of control.

I went to my room and slammed my door. My fists were clenched at my sides while I paced back and forth around the room, trying to catch my breath, and regain my composure. It was taking all of me to keep from going back in the living room and laying hands on her. I heard Briana yelling to Eric on her cell phone for him to come get her before she "fucks me up."

I paid her no mind since it would be a cold day in hell before she whooped my ass. She had gotten lucky with the couple punches she did get. I weighed way more than her and was a lot quicker with my hands. Things could have gotten ugly very quickly if she wasn't my baby sister.

After about ten minutes I went to check on Layla to make sure she was still sleep. Somehow, she had managed to rest through the commotion. I'm glad she was a heavy sleeper. I would have hated for her to see me and her aunt fighting like that. Briana and I had our share of fights in our life, but this one seemed different. We were seriously drifting apart, and it was all behind a man.

<><><>

The next morning, I woke up feeling like awful. I had dozed off on the couch and hadn't even bothered to wrap my hair. Briana had pulled one of my tracks loose, and my head was throbbing. I went to my master bathroom and looked in the mirror. I didn't have a bruise from the punch Briana landed on my face, but I sure looked a mess. I rummaged around in my medicine cabinet until I found my purple wig brush. Along with a little oil, I wrapped my disheveled hair and proceeded to slather on my green mint julep mask. I swore by that mask since I was a teenager. It was cheap, but it got the job done.

It was Saturday, so I figured I would relax most of the afternoon and then take Layla to her dad. He was off on the weekends and had a small apartment in Germantown. I wasn't particularly fond of the area, but I wouldn't deny Layla the quality time she spent with her father. I envied the adoration she displayed for him.

Two o clock rolled around quicker than I had anticipated, and I found myself struggling to get motivated to get out of the house and in route to Germantown.

"Layla do you have your bag ready?" I asked.

"Yes mommy," she responded, dragging *mommy* in a whiney tone.

"What's wrong with you?" I asked, noticing that her normal jovial attitude had been replaced with a somber one.

"Nothing," she replied. I wasn't buying it. Something was up, and I was going to get to the bottom of it.

"Layla, if something is wrong, you know you can tell me right. No matter what it is, you can come to me ... So, what's going on? I know you, and I can tell when you're unhappy."

She hesitated a second, and then her sad demeanor switched to a warmer one.

"Well, I normally like going to my dad's, but he has a new girlfriend and she is over his house a lot. I don't really get to spend as much time with him anymore when I go over there. She has two boys, and they're bad. They fight, and I don't really like being around them ... Do I have to go today? I'd rather stay home and be with you."

I grew angry as my daughter explained her

55

feelings to me. Here I was doing my best to raise her with minimal stress in her life, and Rashid was doing the opposite. He was playing house with some hood-rat, while he was supposed to be spending quality time with his daughter.

"Did one of them hit you?" I asked firmly. My primary concern was that she had not been struck by either of the un-named rug rats. If she said yes, it would be Desert Storm for everybody over there when I arrived.

"No. My dad makes them sit down when he sees them being bad."

"Good. Because your father knows I don't play." I said with a sigh. "And of course, you can stay home honey. I'll talk to your dad and let him know how you feel and that you want to stay home for the weekend. He won't be upset." I hugged her and kissed her on her cheek to reassure her.

I thought about texting Rashid, but I figured he would just try to lie about it and that would further anger me. I would call him later and discuss the issue; for now, I would focus on cheering my baby up.

I called Asia to see if she wanted to join me and Layla at Dave and Buster's with her kids. Our girl's night out had been canceled since Layla decided to stay home, but I figured we could still do something while incorporating our children. I offered to pay for everything since I knew that she was having some financial difficulties. Although she made a good salary at Aetna, her husband wasn't working and was having trouble finding a job. I figured that was the least I could do since she had been listening to my crap for years now.

<><><>

Asia took me up on my offer, so later that evening we met up at Dave and Busters on Christopher Columbus Boulevard in Philly. She of course, brought along her adorable twin boys, Trevor and Tyler. Adorable was an understatement for the two snaggletooth, curly head cuties. Asia and I had margaritas and hot wings, while Layla and the boys ran around the arcade, only returning to get more money for their game cards.

"So, what's been going on girl?" Asia asked. "You been missing in action at Aetna."

"Girl, I still be working. I've just been using a lot of my personal days and vacation time to catch up on some sleep," I laughed. "I just finished repairing a couple properties down in North Philly. So far, I have four. I got them for dirt cheap because they were shells, but it's been very time consuming and labor intensive to fix them up. It's been a challenging adventure," I joked. I usually tried to avoid getting too detailed about my side ventures.

Although Asia was my friend, she was chatty and could be considered nosey at times. Asia was mixed with black and white and had a face full of freckles. She wasn't very attractive, with small lips, big eyes, and a head full of reddish curls. However, what Asia lacked in looks she made up for in personality. She was very bubbly, loving and warm; just like another sister.

"Dang, girl that's awesome. I didn't know you had that many properties. But you've always been good with your money, saving and everything. I'm about to really start saving more; as soon as my income tax check comes back. With two kids and Drew not working, I'm supposed to get back a pretty nice amount," she said with a smile.

Asia's comment about taxes caught me off guard. As much as I loved her, that comment quickly ended the warm and fuzzy thoughts I was just having about her. I quickly grew uncomfortable and began to silently question why she would bring up income taxes. I was one of those people who wore their emotions on their sleeve, well in my case, my face, so I quickly excused myself to run to the bathroom. When I returned I was calm but made a mental note to be a lot more observant of the small circle I kept. I also decided to get off the subject of money and taxes and talk about something else.

When I thought about the people close to me, I noticed that many of them were having money problems; Onney, Asia, and even Briana. At the thought of Briana, I looked down at my phone for the tenth time that day to see if she had called or texted me. Of course, she still hadn't called, and I began to wonder if I went a little overboard with the comment about her boyfriend. Briana had always been a little insecure type, so the comment probably angered her to the max.

After talking with Asia about the incident, she agreed that I had went overboard with my comment and I owed Briana an apology. That still didn't excuse her for hitting me in my house, but like Asia said, why make a remark like that about her boyfriend who she clearly cares for.

"Imagine her saying that about Rashid," Asia said, trying to rationalize the situation.

"Girl please. I wouldn't care, but I do see what you're saying." I agreed with her to a certain extent.

"Then you also have to take into consideration that Briana really looks up to you. I've only met her a few times, but I could tell she does. She obviously wishes she was more like you and when you made that comment you probably triggered jealousy and insecurities from within her. Just call her and apologize. You were wrong for saying what you said, and her attacking you was purely emotional and stemmed from that situation."

"I guess you're right. But that still don't mean she can just haul off hitting people, pulling up my darn tracks," I said, and patted at my hair.

Asia burst out laughing when I said that. I admit, I had to laugh too.

After finding and gathering our worn-out kids, we parted ways. I texted Asia on the way home, thanking her for her insight. I valued our friendship since she was one of the ones who kept it real all the time. She probably knew me better than even Briana did. Nevertheless, I was still being blackmailed by someone close to me, so I would still continue to limit and monitor certain conversation. However, I think it was really time to start talking to Briana about what she may have said drunkenly to one of her girlfriends.

Even though Briana and I were inseparable when we were young, she always had a ton of friends. She was outgoing while I was quieter and more analytical. Although we were both pretty, she was the more charismatic one. That was something I secretly envied. Even as an adult, she oftentimes would have gatherings at her house and invite five or six close girlfriends. I would always opt out, since I had nothing in common with the bar hopping chicks she hung around.

It was becoming more and more likely that one of Briana's friends was probably the culprit. The problem was I knew none of them, and it would be solely up to Briana to determine who it was.

Briana only worked on and off but had a nice row home in the Mt. Airy section of Philadelphia. Anyone not familiar with that section, would know that it's one of the better neighborhoods for African American's in the city. Certain parts of Mt. Airy are home to teachers, doctors and even executives. I'm sure many of her friends were curious as to what she did to afford her the ability to live there, as well as drive a new BMW.

By the time I pulled up to my driveway, Layla was leaning over in the back-seat sleep. A trail of spit went from her face to the seat of my Mustang as she tossed in her sleep. Dave and Busters had worn my baby out. I shook her awake and helped her walk drunkenly into the house. I didn't bother her with undressing since on the weekends, she slept in spurts. I figured she could bathe and brush her teeth in an hour or so when she woke up. I used the opportunity to walk outside and call Rashid. He had been calling and texting me about for hours, regarding when I was bringing Layla by.

"Hey Rashid. We need to talk," I said, as soon as he answered the phone. I figured I would use a calmer approach with this situation. I didn't know how serious he was with this mystery female, or if he knew how uncomfortable Layla was, so I wanted to have facts before I reacted.

"Yeah wassup, and why didn't you bring Layla by? I've been texting and calling you all day."

"Yeah, I saw that, but who's the chick with the Bebe's kids you have around the house when Layla is there?" I asked. I was calm, but I was still aggravated, and I knew it clearly showed.

"Who Kiana? That's just a shorty I was dealing with. Before you flip out though Nijah, let me explain what's going on first ..." Rashid spoke fast, since he knew I was about to let him have it.

"I already know how you feel about females

being around Layla, cuz truthfully I don't want any men around her on ya end. However, she and I are just friends and we aren't serious. She's actually about to get out. Shorty lost her place a couple weeks ago … got evicted or something. I was doing her a favor since I knew her since we were kids. She got those two boys, so I felt sorry for her. She asked me, and I told her she could stay here a week or so until she figured something out. I'm not there like that anyway since I work all the time, and I figured by the time I get there they'd be sleep. I honestly didn't things shit through as far as how it would affect Layla and our weekends together. That is where I messed up, and I apologize to you, and I will definitely apologize to Layla. I love my daughter and I don't want you to or her to ever think anything other than that. I would never put anyone before my daughter."

I paused before responding, since I was growing upset. Even though he had explained and apologized, I still had my reasons.

"First of all, I know you aren't talking about Kiana that used to live around 10th and Diamond? — Booter sister?" I asked with a frown, already knowing the answer.

"Yeah," he responded, slightly embarrassed because of her reputation.

"I just seen her a couple days ago at the Willow Grove mall … probably stealing. Ya trifling ass a trip," I commented.

Booter was an acquaintance of Rashid's. He was

a hood nigga with a hoe for a sister. She wasn't pretty by a long shot, and only had breast and booty going for her. She was a hood-rat with no desire for an education and lived month to month by screwing any nigga moving and living off welfare and S.S.I checks.

"Rashid you have no idea how uncomfortable you made Layla feel. She doesn't know that hoe or her kids. On top of that, she said her boys are bad and they fight, which is no surprise since they mother is Kiana. Luckily, they didn't hit her. What if she had gotten hurt? She didn't even want to go over there today," I said, adding salt to the wound. He sat quietly on the phone, so I continued.

"You really need to use your head when you make decisions. What if I told you that she can't go over there anymore, and your visits would be monitored?" I asked.

He sucked his teeth and the volume in his voice rose. "Then you'd be on some bullshit," he said, ignoring everything else I had just said.

"I'd be on some bullshit because you had a hood-rat around our child? It's about respect Rashid! Respect your daughter and respect her mother!" I shouted, losing my patience, and revealing one of my true reasons for being angry.

Realizing that I was in front of my house in an affluent community, I lowered my voice. I didn't want anyone in my business or thinking I was some big mouthed, ghetto black girl.

"Yo, I already said I messed up. Damn. What the

else you want me to say? I definitely ain't gon sit on the phone and argue with you. That's for sure."

"You know what Rashid. Go to work and save ya money for a lawyer. Cuz ya ass gon need it when I file for sole custody."

"You on some bullshit Nijah!" he accused, while yelling into the phone. "I apologized already and acknowledged my wrongs, but you want to make this about you! What's the real reason you mad?" he asked. I ignored his jealousy accusation like it was nothing.

"Every decision I make; I analyze how it'll affect our daughter. You just admitted that you don't. Until you change that and start putting her first, then you won't see her. Matter of fact, you can see her ... You can see her in a public place, supervised. My lawyer will make sure of that," I threatened.

Rashid paused and then spoke harshly. "You know what Nijah, fuck you! Honestly. You on some corny shit and I'll leave Karma to take care of you."

I hung up the phone in his ear just as he was about to continue his verbal tirade. I didn't give a crap what he said or what he thought. He was out of line for taking Layla to his home to play house with a hoe and her kids. I don't care what the situation was.

Here he was, coming over here professing his love for me in front of Layla, and then taking her to his home where he had a woman and her kids living. It was most certainly confusing her. Hell, it was confusing to me. He was setting bad examples for his young, highly impressionable daughter. That's why females were settling for anything these days. They were constantly being shown and taught that it was normal. Additionally, I was mad about him screwing the community hoe, Kiana.

We would both calm down later, and I would call him, so we could set up a better arrangement for him to spend time with Layla. However, from now on, she would not be going to his home. At the end of the day Rashid wasn't slow. He knew he was wrong, and he would see it from my perspective with a clear head.

<><><>

Hours later, I sat relaxing by my bay window. This was by far, my favorite feature of my home. Plush pillows and cushions aligned the seating space, while expensive purple and gold drapes adorned the large windows. This was my space to read, think, and reflect.

I picked up my phone for the millionth time and checked to see if I had any missed calls. I had several from Rashid, but none from Briana. I decided it was now or never, so I dialed her number to apologize about what I had said. After the second ring, she answered. Knowing Briana, she probably was waiting for *that* call just like I had been.

"Hello?" she answered dryly.

"Hey," I responded. I took an exaggerated deep breath, so she would understand that what I was doing was not easy.

"Listen," I continued. "I know you're probably still mad at me, but at the end of the day we are family. What I said was wrong … I shouldn't have said it. I talked to Asia, and she said the same thing. I didn't mean it, but during the heat of the moment, I had to say something to get under your skin. So, I apologize for that. I understand why you reacted the way you did, but it doesn't take away from the fact that I am your sister, and you can't just go around attacking people."

I waited for her to respond. Ten seconds went by with no response from her. I grew nervous at the thought of rejection.

"Thank you," she said in a sincere tone, surprising me.

"I appreciate the fact that you called and apologized. I look up to you Nijah. You're my big sister. I feel like you pass judgment on me a lot. I'm not perfect and I'm firmly aware of that. It just seems like you are always so quick to let me know that. So, you are calling me apologizing, and saying you were wrong is very dear to me," Briana professed.

"I do apologize for hitting you," she continued. "That wasn't the right way to handle it. I'm sorry … Like I said before, I handle stress different from you and I just snapped. You've been coming down on me hard lately with criticism and it's tough. But I do apologize for my actions, and I just want things to be back to normal."

While I didn't totally agree, I didn't bother to dispute what she was saying. We ended the call with our own set of promises. Briana promised to be more present while we handled our "situation," and I promised to be less critical and more understanding. After talking to Briana, I felt bad. Was I this miserable "hard as nails" type of person? Was I really being the "Negative Nancy" no one wanted to be around? That was who I did not want to be. Wasn't I happy? Or was I?

<><><>

Later that night I found myself wide awake in bed, still pondering over my happiness and future. After all the drinking from Dave and Buster's earlier, plus my nightly wine ritual, I was also wide-awake running to and from the bathroom. As I walked across the plush carpet on my way to my private bath I decided to peek in on Layla. Peering around my home puzzled, I detected a foul odor in the air. I frowned at the stench.

I went to the kitchen and used my foot to press down on my stainless steel, no touch, trash can. When it opened, I cringed from the smell of half eaten cheese dip from Dave and Busters. I immediately began gathering up the bag to take it out back to the dumpster behind my home. I ran to the room and got some sandals before I grabbed the trash.

Opening the door wide, I walked out and into

the back of my yard where I kept the dumpster. After throwing the bag on the side, I turned around and was met by a dark, hooded figure who knocked me hard to the ground. *Thud!* My body jerked as I landed hard on my ass.

Hovering in front of me, the man leaned in to say something, but I quickly scurried back to try to get away. My sandals slid off my feet and I suddenly felt my back hit the dumpster. There was nowhere to run. I wouldn't allow myself to scream, for if I did, I would put Layla in immediate danger also. I didn't want her hearing me, and then running out.

My heart pounded rapidly in my chest, as shock ripped through my body. The intruder used his gloved hand to cover my mouth. With his free hand he grabbed my neck and applied enough pressure to cause me to immediately gasp for air. At that moment, fear cloaked me as I realized I was staring in the face of death. I was going to die right outside in my backyard by the trash, like a stray animal. All I could think of was my daughter Layla searching for me and finding me like that in the morning. Tears welled up in my eyes and made their way down my face.

The masked man suddenly loosened his grip some and leaned into my ear really close to speak.

"I'm here to deliver a message and reminder for you and your sister." His breath was hot and steady.

"The half a million is still due soon. No funny shit. You're easily touchable, *any* and *everywhere*. If you scream or call the police, you'll die next time," he threatened.

He quickly released my neck, and backed away slowly, before cutting through my neighbor's home, and quickly disappearing into the darkness. I didn't realize I had been holding my breath. I let out a deep gasp for air. I was shaking.

The message he brought was very clear; this situation wasn't a game, and whoever the person behind this was, wanted their money as promised. I don't understand why they felt the need to use that type of fear and intimidation to get their point across. Just the thought of going to jail was enough to get us rattled by itself. Whatever the case was, I had one more week left to get the money, no matter what it took.

SIX

MONDAY WAS BACK around, and it was week two of our rapid tax filing spree. Things were still chaotic but weren't as bad as the previous week. I was still working my day job, however, I had rented all of my vacant rooms out, so I wasn't running all around Philadelphia behind potential tenants. I had been looking at a couple larger houses to buy in the Germantown section, however, I would wait before I plunked down money I might later need. Additionally, making many of the homes livable required a great deal of time that I just didn't have at the moment. I was doing any and everything possible to stay focused and keep my mind off the terrible situation I was in.

Throughout all of the adversity in my life, I still kept my sights on one day owning dozens of rental properties in the city. Once I reached that goal, I would branch out and start attacking other forms of real estate, like office buildings and complexes.

Briana was alone and on time tonight, so we were able to get started promptly. I didn't tell her or Onney about what had happened the previous night with the intruder. The whole incident had me extremely fearful and very cautious. I figured I would carry that burden alone so they both could at least sleep through the night. I also told myself that as soon as this was over, I would be selling my beloved townhouse and moving to a gated community where stuff like that would never happen.

We had half of the two hundred refunds done and were right on schedule to have the other hundred done by the end of the week. With that being said, my fingers ached from typing, and my eyes were constantly red and tingling from lack of sleep.

With some minor manipulations on the tax forms, we were able to get higher returns on many of them. The adjustments would allow us to see around $600-$700Gs. We planned to pay off the other four fifty and pocket the rest. This would be our last run, so we had to make it count for something.

"So, Briana what do you plan to do after this?" I asked, just making small talk.

"Girl, I don't know. I'll probably take $30,000 and finally pay for hair school," she said, still focused on the laptop screen.

Briana had been doing weaves since we were teenagers. She wasn't the best braider but that was something she knew could be learned.

"Awesome," I responded, in a surprised manner. I was actually surprised that she had been considering going back to school for something.

"You'll do great with that. You know ya curls always be on point. Especially those wand curls you be doing ... Get that braiding down and you'll kill em in Philly on the weave tip."

Philly was known as the hair mecca of the country. Chick's lived and died for weaves and braids. It was common to see a young female at the bus stop with a $300-$400 weave. Chick's would buy a weave before they put the money towards a computer or car. Senseless, but nevertheless it was facts.

"And you know I got ya back financially if you decide to open a shop ... I ain't rich, but I got a lil something put up to the side where I could comfortably help you out."

Briana smiled brightly. "Thanks, Nijah. I'll definitely take you up on that offer. I already know what I'm gonna call it ... Baddies, short for "Bad Bitches," she laughed.

I rolled my eyes and laughed while responding. "Only you would name a salon some ghetto shit like that," I joked.

"Oh! Guess who I seen! I forgot to tell you," she revealed excitedly.

"Mommy's sister, Aunt Sheena. She was cleaned up and working at McDonald's, down Broad and Allegheny."

"Broad and Allegheny? Why were you way down there?" I frowned. "Well whatever, how was she?"

I quickly reminded myself that my protective, inquisitive ways could come across as overbearing and critical, so I stopped myself when asking why Briana was way on Allegheny in North Philly. Here we were, almost thirty years old and I was questioning her about her whereabouts like a kid. I had to stop doing that.

"I was with Eric. He lives in North Philly remember? We had sat down to eat, and she was working the counter. She looked so good. She had some fake teeth in, and she had gained weight and everything. In fact, I gave her my number and I'm going to pick her up tomorrow when she gets off. She says she been at a half-way house and had been locked up for five years. I pray she stay straight. I would love to have her around. She reminds me so much of mommy. You should come by with Layla."

I wasn't sure what to think of reconnecting with my mother sister, Aunt Sheena. A part of me felt like I should be angry because we were in and out of foster homes while she was running around getting high. However, another part of me, the grown-up part of me, understood that she had an addiction that she couldn't control.

I agreed to go by Briana's and see Aunt Sheena. I would not bring up the past. What happened, happened, and I would only move forward. I had been trying to apply that concept to every aspect of my life, including with Rashid.

The day after our argument I spoke with him. He agreed that if he ever decided to get serious with someone, he would discuss it with me before Layla met her. The same would go for me. Rashid however, insisted that would never be the case, because we would eventually get back together. Highly unlikely, but I was no fortune teller, so I just let him talk.

<><><>

The next evening, I pulled up to Briana's house around 6:15. I had just picked Layla up from school and made a pit stop to the supermarket, so Layla could make a ridiculously large salad at the salad bar. I hated when she ate in my car, but my baby was hungry, so she would not be deprived.

I didn't see Briana's car in the yard, so I called her to make sure she was home. She answered on the first ring.

"Hey Nijah! We're in the house. The door is open."

"Ok cool, where's your car?" I asked.

She paused. "Oh, Eric has it. His is in the shop," she lied.

"Oh ok, boo. Well we're coming in now."

I hung up the phone and rolled my eyes. I told Briana that the nigga Eric was a leech. There probably wasn't anything wrong with his car; he was probably riding around fronting and flossing in her BMW like it was his. Hopefully he wouldn't tear it up. The last car she had, an all-white 2013 Dodge Charger, had been wrecked by a former boyfriend.

We walked into Briana's home and Layla greeted her with a warm hug. She adored Briana and I wished Briana would spend more time with her. Aunt Sheena sat in the dining area and stood up nervously to greet us. She had tears in her eyes and appeared anxious but happy, like she just found her long lost family member. In reality, she actually had.

"Oh, my goodness," she gushed. "You look exactly the same. Still beautiful, but all grown up," she exclaimed emotionally, before reaching out her large arms to embrace me.

I opened my arms to give her a hug. She reminded me so much of my mother. The physical resemblance was uncanny. Aunt Sheena was full-figured just like my mother had been. Even though she had been on drugs all those years, she never became extremely skinny like most addicts. The woman standing before me looked good. She had all her weight back and looked well put together, with false teeth, and her hair neatly curled under.

"Hey Aunt Sheena. I'm so happy to see you. We missed you."

Emotions overwhelmed me, and I quickly realized how much I missed having a mother figure in my life. I hoped to get that back with Aunt Sheena. Lord knows we all needed her in our life. I looked to my side and Briana was crying silent tears. We were all so happy.

Aunt Sheena got acquainted with everyone while we played catch up and ate some wing dings Briana had fried. Aunt Sheena quickly took a liking to Layla, continuously hugging her and pinching her cheeks. Our visit was very emotional, yet happy. However, it was cut short because Aunt Sheena had to be back at the half-way house by 9. Since Eric wasn't back yet, we all piled up in my Mustang and I dropped her off.

The whole time Briana was constantly calling Eric to see where he was. Of course, he wasn't answering, and when he finally did, he claimed he wasn't getting good reception and had been tied up. I pretended not to notice. These days it was better for me to just mind my business. I didn't want to get punched again.

We all said bye to Aunt Sheena while we exchanged numbers, promising to keep in touch. I had every intention of doing so. With her being straight, she gave off such a warm motherly vibe that I desperately needed. Time would tell whether she stayed straight or not, however, after five years in prison you would think that she would. I could only go off of what she said she wanted.

<><><>

The week was going by smoothly and things were looking up. I had only been contacted once from our blackmailer about the money. For some reason the voice sounded a little different from last time. Maybe my mind was playing tricks on me.

Aunt Sheena was still coming around after work and had been keeping in contact with everyone via phone calls and texts daily, sometimes multiple times a day. Briana was even considering inviting her to come live with her after she got out of the half-way house in a few months.

Even though things were going smoothly, I still was extra tired. More so, because Briana hadn't been feeling well lately. She would go to the bathroom multiple times while we were working and complained of stomach and headaches. I prayed to God she wasn't pregnant by that fool Eric. I had let her go home twice, and I just stayed up later to make up for her not being there. I would be glad when all this crap was over. I typically didn't require a lot of sleep, but lately I was truly deprived, running off a couple of hours.

Later during the week while I was working at Aetna, my dear friend, Asia stopped to talk to me at my cubicle.

"Hey Nijah. You been alright lately?" she asked, appearing a bit concerned.

"I'm good girl. Just been running around lately and haven't been getting as much sleep," I replied, with a light yawn.

As Asia leaned against the manufactured wall that enclosed my cubicle, I noticed her new diamond tennis bracelet. It sparkled gently and looked like it cost a pretty penny.

"Dang Asia boo. I see you blinged out. When you get that?" I asked.

"Oh, I meant to tell you about this," she said, smiling. She pulled her arm away from the cubicle and started to examine the bracelet, turning it on her arm.

"Drew got it for me," she said, referring to her husband. "He was offered a job Monday that pays really well. We all went out to dinner to celebrate and he surprised me with this. I'm not even sure how he paid for it. I didn't ask. Probably charged it on his credit card. We went through a really rough patch these past couple of months and he said he appreciated me for being there for him and never judging."

"Well it's beautiful," I admitted. "Guard it with ya life, or else I might steal it," I joked, laughing.

"Aight girl, well I was just checking on you. I'ma call you later and we can play catch up. Plus, you never told me if you apologized or not. I'm gone though, I'ma call you." She walked off and left me with some unanswered questions.

Asia hadn't been acting strange or anything, but it seemed like she could be hiding something. Her bracelet looked like it had cost at least a grand, so why hadn't she told me about it. Most women would have jumped at the chance to brag to their friends about the new, diamond bracelet their husband had bought for them. And that was a pretty hefty price for Drew to pay for a bracelet, even if it did go on his credit card. I didn't know if Asia was being 100% honest, but I did know that I would definitely keep my eyes open for wolves dressed in sheep's clothing.

SEVEN

I WAS NORMALLY up by 5am so I would have more than enough time to drop Layla off and be on time to work in Blue Bell by 7am. This morning was different. The sound of my ringing phone woke me abruptly out of my sleep. By the time I clumsily reached for the phone, the ringing had stopped. It was 4am. I had just laid down at 3:15 and I was dog tired. My burning eyes struggled to stay open as I slowly sat up in the bed to check my phone. I had several missed calls from a private number, another missed call from Onney, who had called me around 1am. I wasn't sure how I had managed to miss her call since I was still up at that time.

Just as I was erasing my call log, my phone began to ring again. I answered the call on the second ring.

"Hello?" I asked tiredly, into the phone.

"Hi, is this Nijah Washington?" a stern, Caucasian sounding voice asked.

"Yes, this is. Who is this?" I asked, a bit puzzled and confused. I wondered why someone who sounded like a telemarketer would be calling at this time of night.

"Ms. Washington, my name is Detective Carl Leonard. It's about your sister Onnye Washington," he explained. Onney had never changed her maiden name.

"Yes. What's going on officer?" I was now fully awake and was growing scared and confused.

"Well you were listed as next of kin for Ms. Washington. I'm sorry to tell you this, but we found her several hours ago. — She's dead. ... apparently from suicide."

My body grew numb and I suddenly lost my breath. I couldn't scream, I couldn't cry. I was mute. I felt like my life was crumbling around me and I was trapped. I dropped the phone and curled into a ball. Five minutes later, reality sunk in and I was crying like a baby. *Why was everything happening? What did we do that was so wrong?*

At the time I couldn't answer those questions, but I did know that I needed to figure what was going on in my life and get a grip on things. I didn't know if things could get any worse. In all actuality things were just beginning.

<><><>

I don't remember the four-hour drive to Onney's home. Neither Briana or I, were emotionally stable enough to drive, so Eric offered to take us. Even though we weren't super close to Onney, we were still sisters. I had become closer to her more recently with all that had been going on. Aunt Sheena couldn't go since she had to work and any deviance from her routine could be a violation, so we all agreed it was best not to risk it. She told us to keep her updated with texts and she would call when she could.

When we pulled up to Onney's home the scene was surreal. The house had yellow, plastic crime scene tape around it, and there were police everywhere. As I tried to enter the home, I was stopped by several uniformed officers who were guarding the area. I asked to speak with Detective Leonard, who came out in several minutes to usher me and Briana in. As we followed the detective, I peered around the inside of Onney's home and realized she hadn't been very honest with me about her financial situation. Her home was quite lavish for a Lieutenant's salary at a correctional facility. I wondered how she had been holding on this long.

We walked into an empty bedroom where Detective Leonard closed the door and finally begin to speak.

"I'm sorry we had to meet under these circumstances, but I'm Detective Leonard. You're Nijah?" he asked, extending his hand to me. He then looked over to Briana.

"And you miss lady, I'm sorry I didn't get your name."

"Oh hi. I'm Briana Washington. Onnye's youngest sister," she replied, in a low weary tone.

"Well ladies, it appears to have been a suicide. She used a gun that was registered to her husband. He was at work when it happened. Of course, we called and confirmed that information. He works the 11p-11a shift over at the prison. That ruled him out as a suspect. A neighbor heard the gunshot and called it in. It looks as if your sister was going through some issues with depression. She has a prescription made out to her in her purse. Her husband didn't even know about it.

I wasn't surprised by what he was saying. It all started to make sense. She had said she was going through other things, and it was a lot on her.

"The main reason I brought you in here today however, was because although your sister was going through depression, she was also under investigation at work. She was suspended yesterday pending the outcome of investigation." He studied our faces closely to watch for a reaction.

"Oh my god," we both gasped. "For what?"

"Well, apparently she had been accessing private inmate information and using it inappropriately. The investigation is still on-going, but from what I was told, there was a possibility that criminal charges would be filed."

I felt as if I had been hit in the gut with a sledgehammer. *Onney had taken her life because someone had found out she had been accessing prisoner information.* There's no telling what else they knew. The feeling of guilt flowed through my body, so I placed my hands over my face and shook my head while I cried silent tears. Briana stood there stunned as well. As much as I wanted to cry out in true sorrow, I couldn't: it would look too suspicious.

"Ladies I am sorry for your loss. If there's anything I can do to help you, or if you have any questions, please call me. I'll give you two a moment alone to gather yourself. I'm sure you're ready to begin making arrangements for her."

He handed me his business card while I lifted my head up long enough to thank him and take the card.

I looked at Briana and said nothing. The look I gave her confirmed that we had a whole lot to discuss. However, Onney's house was definitely not the place to do it. Lord knows who was listening.

Before we left, I went to speak to Onney's husband Kevin, who was sitting in the kitchen answering more questions from detectives. After they finished speaking, I gave him a hug and explained to him that although I didn't know him, I was there if he needed me. He gave me his number, so I could help him make arrangements for Onney. I could tell he had been drinking but I said nothing. I wasn't there to judge. Everyone was hurting and we all would deal with it in our own way, just like we dealt with the hidden sorrows and skeletons within us; whatever they were.

<><><>

The week that followed was very emotional and hectic. We laid Onney to rest in a small, quiet ceremony in the town she lived in. The turnout was small since she didn't have much family, however, a few loyal friends from her job showed up to pay their respects. According to her husband, many of her fellow officers did not show up because of the scandal surrounding the investigation. Of course, Onney's husband walked around intoxicated most of the day, however he was still respectful and helped me lay my sister down to rest properly.

Briana of course was a nervous wreck when she did finally decide to publicly mourn. She too, kept her emotions in check with the help of alcohol.

When I laid down to bed the night of the funeral, I prayed to Onney, and I prayed to God, asking them both for forgiveness. I felt nothing but sadness and guilt behind getting Onney involved with this scam of mine. There was no way that I would file another single tax return that was illegal. I had made most of the money for the blackmail to end, and whatever I didn't have I would take it out of my account. All I could pray for, was that whoever was doing this would let me move forward, and that the IRS didn't catch up with us. I had learned my lesson. I was thankful for what I had. I had been humbled. I felt guilt. What more could they ask of me?

A month had passed since Onney's suicide, and I still struggled daily with grief and feelings of guilt. While dealing with that, Briana and I were at odds once again. Lately, she had returned to acting odd and very distant. I would call her, and she would call me back, *days* later. I would stop by her home, and she would not answer the door; even when her car was there. She always pretended she had been sleeping. I knew a lie when I heard one. When I did manage to catch her, she would run back and forth to the bathroom in fifteen-minute increments. If I didn't know any better, she was either pregnant, or god forbid, on drugs.

While I was deep in thought, I turned left off Broad Street to the parking lot of McDonald's, at Broad and Allegheny. I was there to pick up Aunt Sheena from work, so we could go have an early dinner before her curfew at the half-way house she was staying at. She was due to be released from there in a week, and I wanted to talk to her about her next move.

I looked down at my watch and it was 6:02 pm. I knew Aunt Sheena would be walking out any second. She didn't like working at McDonald's and when it was time for her to leave, she didn't play any games. Right on cue, she walked out the door, smoothing her ponytail out after taking off her work hat.

"Dang Aunt Sheena, you didn't even bother to

change." I laughed, before giving her a kiss on the cheek.

"Girl, I ain't got time for that!" she argued with a laugh. "I was ready to go. Them fools was getting on my damn nerves today too," she huffed.

"Where we headed?" she asked, still trying to fix her mashed-in hat hair.

"Well, I was just going to go Downtown so we could eat. I wanted to talk to you about something anyway.

"Aight cool. I don't want to be too far from the half-way house anyway, since I gotta be in by nine." She looked down at her stained uniform. "I'll change this mess in the bathroom. I got my clothes in my bag."

Aunt Sheena sure could be ghetto as hell, but I loved every bit of her. She always kept it real and never sugar coated anything.

Where's Layla?" she asked, after looking in the empty back seat.

"She's with her dad. Ever since Onney passed he has been staying some nights at my house to help me out. He's off on the weekends, so hum being around helps me get a lot done."

Aunt Sheena looked at me with a smirk on her face. "Mmmmm hmmm...I see somebody back over there knocking them boots out," she joked.

If I was light-skinned my face would have turned blood red. My aunt sure knew she would say any darn thing. Over the past month we all had grown comfortable together, and Aunt Sheena was proving to be just as outspoken as she wanted to be. She was truly, a unique piece of work.

"Naa Auntie. It's not like that. He really is helping me out," I smiled. She wasn't buying it. She cut her eyes at me once again, causing me to grin. I couldn't help but love her.

<><><>

Aunt Sheena and I got a small booth in a quiet section in the back of Applebee's. We both ordered the parmesan sirloin and drank Strawberry lemonade while we waited for our food to come.

"So, what did you want to talk to me about?" Aunt Sheena asked, initiating small talk, since I had been quiet since we arrived.

"Well I don't know how to put this." I paused. "I know it's kind of a sensitive subject for you — but recently I've noticed Briana's been acting weird." Aunt Sheena raised her eyebrows in curiosity. I continued.

Maybe you've noticed it too ... she barely answers the phone or returns calls. When I am able to get up with her, she acts really weird, running back and forth to the bathroom ... and most recently she hasn't been keeping up on her appearance. She looks like crap, and her hair was a wreck last time I saw her. That is not like my sister — I think something's going on with her. Maybe she's pregnant, depressed, or worse … on drugs." I waited for her to respond.

Aunt Sheena shook her head in dismay. "I knew it … I saw it over a month ago when she came to pick me up from work one day. She seemed spaced out. I peeped the signs, but I dismissed them because it was Briana and I didn't want to believe it. If she is on drugs, it's because of the Eric. I been meaning to tell you where I remembered him from. I just could never find the right time." She paused before continuing.

"You may have about it, but about six years ago, before I went to prison, there was some stick-up kids running around Philadelphia robbing drug houses. Well, Eric had a couple of them in West Philly … Yeah, he's a dealer and I knew of him through my time on the streets," she confirmed. "Well, one night one of his houses got ambushed and his cousin was murdered. According to the streets, Eric went on a rampage and killed about four people who were involved with his cousin's death, including a pregnant female. He ended up getting locked up but beat the charges. The witness never showed up to testify. From the stories I've heard, he's ruthless. I personally didn't know him, but he was very well known through the city. His case was all over the news." She shook her head.

I stared at Aunt Sheena in disbelief. "I'm sure Briana has no idea."

"Nijah baby, one thing you gotta understand about Briana is, she's a big girl and is going to do what she wants. That boy got her gone over him. She out here doing whatever he's doing ... That's why she's acting so different. She's in love with him and he can't do no wrong in her eyes. That's something that you're not going to be able to come in between. You see how fast she knocked you upside ya head over something you said about him ... so, imagine trying to get him out the picture. You also gotta remember that she's 26, not sixteen. You can't tell her what to do." I sighed uncomfortably.

Briana is a lot like your mother and I were. She's weak minded and she looks for love in the wrong places. It doesn't help that she didn't get much of it when she was younger. For that, I blame your mother and myself ... With that being said, you're not going to be able to compete with the man she thinks she's in love with. The best way to be there for Briana is to never let her get too distant, stay in contact with her, and as hard as it may seem, never speak ill of Eric," she said with a serious face.

I stared at Aunt Sheena for a second and then picked up my glass to take a sip of lemonade to get rid of the lump that had formed in my throat. At the end of the day, Aunt Sheena was right. There wasn't much I could do but talk to Briana. I would confront her about her potential drug problem, but I would do it when the time was right. For now, I would pray to God and beg for his mercy for my sister.

<><><>

During the drive home I realized I had never talked to Aunt Sheena about her living arrangements for the upcoming week. Although I loved my aunt, I wasn't sure about her living with me because of Layla. I instead, had been thinking about offering her some space at one of my properties.

My largest property in North Philly had a basement that I could have converted and livable in a week. I would just get one of my guys to add some carpet. I had intended on renting that out as a studio since the plumbing was in order to add a kitchenette. Surprisingly, the previous owner had installed a small, but functional bathroom. I guess they had the same ideas as me. I figured it would be perfect for Aunt Sheena if she wanted it.

I took a detour from my home and decided to go by Briana's to check on her. It was a little after nine, so I knew she would be up. Before I got out of my car I called her phone, but of course there was no answer. Seeing her car, I got out and went and knocked on the door. Not surprisingly, a male answered.

I recognized the brown-skinned guy from the casino the night Briana met Eric. He smiled flirtatiously when he opened the door.

"How you doing baby?" he asked. I could smell weed permeating off his clothes. I held my breath to keep from visibly cringing. I hope the smell didn't somehow jump off him and find its way to my body.

"I'm fine — my sister home?" I asked, barely letting myself in the house through the small space he had made at the doorway.

"Yeah she here," Eric said, standing up when I walked in the door. I'll go get her for you," he offered.

"No that's okay, I want to go back and show her something." I didn't bother to ask his permission to walk through my sister's house. I didn't feel the need to, regardless of who he thought he was. Besides, I was trying to hurry up and get to the back of the room with Briana. The sight of Eric made my skin crawl.

I quickly made my way to Briana's bedroom. To my surprise, she wasn't in there. When I turned around to walk out, I noticed Eric had followed me in the room. He closed the door behind him and locked it.

"Where's Briana?" I asked, while looking to the door. "I thought you told me she was in here." I grew instantly afraid. The sight of Eric and knowing he was a murderer was giving me the creeps. I was shook.

"Why would you lock the door?" I asked.

"I just wanted to talk to you about something." He smiled, while running his hand over his head of surprisingly neat cornrows.

"Ok. Well talk. And you can open the door to do that," I said, glancing back over to the doorway.

Ignoring my request, he began to speak. "So, I heard from Briana that you don't like me."

"I never said I didn't like you," I answered, keeping the conversation to a minimum. I wondered why she would tell him something like that.

"For some reason, I don't believe you," he responded, with another smirk.

"It's a shame too," he continued, "because you would really enjoy my company if you got to know me." He then did the unexpected and rubbed his crotch lustfully while looking me up and down.

Before I responded, I inconspicuously reached in my purse and felt to see if I had my mace. I knew if something went down, it wouldn't do much, but at this point, it was all I had available.

"Let me get something straight with you Eric … You're right. I don't care very much for you. A lot of guy's my sister runs into are users. Briana has a little more than the average chick and I've seen countless men, like yourself, try to take advantage of that. It's also inappropriate and disgusting gestures like the one you just made, that makes me care even less for you … Now I don't want no beef with you, but I'd appreciate if you open the door, and let me be on my way."

Somewhere inside of me I had the courage to just say what I said. In all actuality, Eric had me terrified. I made eye contact with him while I waited for his response.

He smirked and then unlocked and opened the door. He still didn't move, so I brushed past him on my way out. The whole time he blatantly stared me up and down shaking his head in satisfaction. I regretted wearing the curve hugging dress I had just bought from The Pink Elephant.

I made my way out of Briana's house while Eric's two friends made kissing sounds and cat-calls. I called Briana's phone as soon as I got in my car; of course, she didn't answer. I told her to call me but left the part out about Eric talking slick to me at her house. She wouldn't believe me anyway, and even if she did, she would take his side before mine. I chalked it up and decided, with Briana, some things were better left unsaid when it pertained to Eric.

<><><>

When I got home, Layla was sleep and Rashid was in the living room watching television. He'd been there since Onney had passed, and, he made me feel much safer. I plopped down beside him after saying hi and kicked off my heels. I had a long day.

"I see you found my liquor stash," I laughed, after noticing the small glass he had, that appeared to be filled with vodka and orange juice.

"Yeah, Layla wore me out. It's some pizza in the kitchen if you want some," he offered. He couldn't cook so he ordered. *At least he tried*, I thought to myself. I smelled the alcohol on his breath and quickly realized he hadn't *just* started drinking: he had been drinking for quite some time.

"I'm okay Rashid, I took Aunt Sheena out to

Applebee's." I yawned lightly. "I'm gonna go take a shower and hop in bed. I'm tired. Don't forget to cut the T.V off."

"Aight," Rashid responded, looking up at me with glossy eyes. I could tell he was almost drunk. Surprisingly, he never really could handle much liquor. If he was going to do drugs he should stick to weed.

<><><>

I was sleep when I felt someone crawl into my bed. When I felt the strong hands grab my waist, I realized it wasn't Layla: it was Rashid. My heart instantly began to pound; however, it wasn't from fear; it was from arousal.

"Rashid what are you doing?" I asked, my breathing accelerating. I already knew what he had come for.

"Shhhhhh," he whispered drunkenly into my ear. "Relax. I just want you for tonight. I promise I won't say nothing else to you about us … just give me tonight," he whispered passionately. He leaned over me, kissed my chin, and pulled down my panties. I wanted to say no, but I remained silent. My mind was mute, but my body was melting.

My mouth just would not open to respond. My body spoke for me, and Rashid took full advantage. He licked and sucked on my nipples until they stood firm and hard against his toned chest. He gently and lovingly kissed every part of my body, not missing a spot. What we were doing wasn't right, *or was it?* Right or wrong, it felt too good to stop, and I was long overdue for what he was about to give me.

Rashid sucked my toes, and then made his way up my legs and thighs with his tongue. He stopped right in my center, which I exposed fully for him. Grabbing my thighs to scoot me down, he then sucked and licked at my throbbing pearl until it was wet and continuously producing a warm trickle of womanly juices. I shuddered from delight. Just as I was about to cum, I pushed his head away and he rose up, eagerly stuffing all nine hard inches of himself inside of me.

Rashid screwed me hard and good that night. When the morning came, reality struck for me, and I asked myself what mess I had just created.

EIGHT

IT WAS FINALLY the first week of May, and right on schedule, I had been getting a call almost every day from the blackmailer about the upcoming deposit. Most of the money from the returns had already been direct-deposited into the multiple accounts I owned. Because it was such a large deposit, I was instructed to spread the transactions out over multiple accounts.

I was ready to get the deposits done so I could move on with my life. I called Briana and she agreed to be ready by ten in the morning, so we could head to Bank of America early. A week before, I had informed her it was important for her to be reachable since this was such an important matter.

Things had started to look up in my life. Rashid and I were getting along well, and I was considering a reconciliation with him. Aunt Sheena was out of the half-way house and was living at my studio apartment in North Philly. She was doing very well with work and staying clean. I was enormously proud of her and having her in my life was a huge blessing. She filled a void I never knew existed. We also hadn't heard anything about the investigation from Onney's job, which was a huge relief. I had also been hanging out with Asia more. With her husbands' new job, she had even been picking up the tabs during our quick get-togethers.

I pulled up to Briana's home at 9:55 am. Since I was a little early, I decided to go in to wait for her, instead of waiting in the car. I knocked on the door and wasn't surprised when it took Briana five minutes to answer it. I didn't say anything; I just gave her a look to hurry up. I noticed Briana had bags under her eyes and looked extremely tired. As usual, she raced through her house, this time in sweat pants and a t-shirt, trying to get ready so we could leave.

"Hey Briana!" I called to her. "I'm going to use the bathroom while you finish getting ready." I had to pee after drinking a large Iced Coffee.

I quickly used Briana's notoriously messy, half bathroom, and flicked my hands dry in the sink after washing the. "Briana you got some lotion?" I yelled out again. She was in her powder room getting ready, so I went into her bedroom to get some lotion since I hadn't brought in my purse. I knew exactly where she kept hers; right out in the open.

Briana's room was also a mess. On her dresser

was about a dozen bottles of Victoria's Secret lotions, all half used. Today, they were covered by a thick stack of wrinkled papers. Being nosey, I picked them up to read them. Quickly scanning them, I thought I was seeing things. *It can't be*, I thought. *No way*. I wiped my eyes and looked again to be sure. Instantly my heart raced, and the uncontrollable feeling of rage began to form within my body.

I couldn't believe my eyes, but they sure weren't lying to me. The papers were from Bank of America, and they were the welcome papers for the three new accounts made out to Briana Washington and Eric Smith. I pulled out my phone to confirm that my mind wasn't playing tricks on me. Sure enough, the account numbers matched those that had been sent to me by the blackmailer.

The anger I felt was at once replaced with hurt when I confirmed what I already knew. I truly couldn't believe it. The account numbers in my phone, matched those on the papers I was holding. The same papers I had picked up off my sister's desk. Briana was the blackmailer. I had to break it down in my mind, so it could register. I couldn't believe that my own *sister* was extorting me for money. I left out the room feeling sick to my stomach, but not before grabbing the papers. I was going to confront my so-called sister.

<><><>

"Briana what is this?" I asked, storming into the powder room where she was putting on makeup to fix her disheveled appearance. My voice was laced with anger and I had started to tremble from the emotions building up in my body.

"What?" she asked confused, while using her hand to block the stack of papers I had just unexpectedly hurled into her face.

"Bank of America papers Briana?" I asked her. My facial expression was distorted with the look of hurt plastered on it. I stood in the doorway of the powder room and waited for an explanation from her. Thirty seconds passed, and that explanation never came. Instead, Briana stood there like a kid being chastised and no explanation of why they did what they did.

"How could you blackmail your own sister?" I asked painfully, my voice trembling. "On top of that … you kept up this ridiculous scheme, even after Onney took her own life behind it!" She stared at me scared. with tears welling up in her eyes.

"Onney died behind this Briana!" I screamed. "Because of you!" Words couldn't express the way I felt. Still standing in the doorway my heart beat rapidly, sweat formed on my nose, and my mind was giving me silent instructions to hit Briana.

"I — I don't know Nijah," she cried, with a confused look on her face. "I didn't mean for any of it to happen. Please let me explain. I — I — It's not my fault. I'm messed up." She ran her hand over her head and sobbed. "I overspent … and I didn't know how to come to you … plus Eric said …" she stammered, visibly shaken.

"Eric said what! To stab ya sister in the back! … Why Briana? Explain that," I begged to know, my voice cracking. Still no answer, so I continued my tirade.

"Because you're selfish! Do you have any idea what this has done to me? Done to Onney? Her husband!? Of course, you don't! Because all you care about is yourself and Eric … All you care about is feeding your damn drug habit!" She looked at me with guilt and anguish laced on her face.

"Oh, what you didn't think anyone knew?" I asked in disbelief. "You walk around looking like shit. Running back and forth to the bathroom to get high. He got you looking stupid and he's out here living his life, using you for every penny he can get from you. You wouldn't have seen much of that money, because he would've used it up or been gone with it."

"Ni Ni Nijah, I'm sorry," she cried, walking towards me.

"Don't come near me," I spat, walking backwards out of her reach. We weren't kids anymore and she wasn't just going to do whatever she wanted to me and I forgive her like I usually did. This was the ultimate level of deceit. *This* was different.

"You sent someone to my house … my home where I rest my head with my *child*, to muscle me … Your own sister … You ain't shit Briana, and if you weren't my sister I'd pound on you." I slammed my fist into my other open hand for emphasis.

"I'm so sorry Nijah! I swear. Let me explain," she pleaded.

Her pleas however, were ignored. I didn't want to hear anything she had to say. I had to leave quickly before I did something I would regret.

I shook my head from side to side and responded, "No you're not Briana. You're sorry you got caught. But you reap what you sow sister," I said, with venom dripping from my voice. I looked at her with rage in my eyes and continued.

"Starting now, you're dead to me. Live and die with ya choices."

I shook my head in disgust and turned around to walk out of the room. Briana fell into her chair and sobbed, but I didn't care. She could rot in hell for all I cared.

My sister wasn't crying because she had wronged someone else and felt guilty. She was crying because of her own situation. There would be no money, because she had been caught. In my mind, Briana was the lowest of the low. What kind of person would continue with blackmail when they lost their sister behind it? Right now, I had to get away from her before I wound up doing something I regretted. I vowed that I would not allow my life to crumble at the hands of another. I had to do what I had to do for Nijah, since others were doing it all for da doe.

I had no idea that this was the beginning of more

to come. Had I known what was headed my way, I would have run fast away from Philadelphia. The drama wasn't over just yet; in fact, it had just begun.

PART 2

ONE

FOUR MONTHS HAD passed since I found out my own sister was blackmailing me for money. I tried not to think about it, since at times it was hard to digest. I hadn't spoken to Briana since the day I had stormed out of her house, after finding account information that proved she was the cause of my unraveling life. It had taken everything out of me to keep from beating her ass half to death. The saying is true: *Just because they're blood doesn't make them family.*

My Aunt Sheena, who had recently come back into our life, was still in contact with Briana even though she had done what she had done. She refused to write her off, vowing to love her unconditionally. I too still loved her unconditionally, but I chose to love her with no contact. Some people you could have in your heart, but not in your life, and it would be a freezing day in hell before she was allowed back in my life.

Ever since I was a girl, my life had been affected from either the mistakes of others or trying to help others. For years, I had been living for everyone else. It was time for me to make myself happy and start living for Nijah. I refused to let Briana's hatred and jealousy consume me or my life. I was a firm believer in choosing who you allowed into your circle and life, family or not.

As much as I disliked my sister at the time her true colors were revealed, I still chose to remain fair. There was no way in hell I was depositing a half a million in her account after I found out it was going to her and her shady boyfriend Eric. However, I did give her what she was entitled to: half. The scheming trick sure wasn't getting a penny more.

Many people in a situation like ours would have just kept everything and wouldn't have given her a dime. I on the other hand, wasn't like that. I believed in karma. Even though I was wronged by my sister, I knew her guilt would eat away at her, and so would Karma.

The worst thing about the whole ordeal, was that our oldest sister Onney had ended up taking her life while Briana was scamming us. Unbeknownst to us, Onney had been on depression medications. Somehow her job found out she had been accessing prisoner information that we were using for our scam, and she was later put under investigation. Onney knew everything was about to hit the fan and took her life so she wouldn't have to face it. I guess she felt like she had dealt with enough in her life, and enough was enough.

Despite Onney committing suicide, Briana continued her scheme during such a vulnerable time. She had no remorse even as Onney lay lying cold in her grave. The only reason she stopped was because she had been caught. Guilt still ate away at me every day about my role in Onney's death. I often wondered if it ate at Briana.

Layla suddenly appeared in the room and removed me from my not so fond memories.

"Mommy, you have a missed call from Aunt Sheena. I heard it ring but I couldn't get to it quick enough," Layla said, while extending the phone to me with her chubby hands. I took the phone quietly while she quickly scurried back to her room.

"Thanks baby," I replied, before she made it fully out the door. Looking down at the phone, I saw that I had *several* missed calls from Aunt Sheena. I wondered what she wanted. I dialed her number. The sound of her standard ringtone blared into my ears as

I waited for her to answer the phone. After four rings she finally picked up.

"Hey Nijah boo," my Aunt Sheena greeted me warmly in the receiver. "I almost missed your call, I was washing my hands." I could hear the warm smile in her voice, as well as the water still running in the background.

"Wassup with you Auntie? Everything ok?" I asked.

"Just calling to check up on you and Lay." She paused as if she wanted to say something but was hesitant. "I saw Briana today … She called me, and I met her after work. I figured you wouldn't want her around the house," she said, referring to my studio apartment she lived in.

I remained silent. After-all, Aunt Sheena was praying for a response that I was not about to give her.

"Nijah when you gon at least sit down and talk to Briana? At least to get some damn answers? Don't you want to know what the hell was going on inside her head when she did what she did? I'm not saying you must kiss and make up, I'm just saying that something terribly wrong happened, and she owes you an explanation. Then you can move on. I know you love your sister. You two share a bond."

"Is she still with Eric?" I asked, rolling my eyes, and disregarding the speech she just gave. I didn't want to hear the sermon right now.

"She says she's still seeing him, but she is trying

to get her life back on track. I know what I'm about to tell you doesn't make it any better, but Briana also struggled with depression. She never told you, but she was on meds too. You know like she does, going from foster home to foster home wasn't easy. She felt abandoned and she felt unloved. She doesn't know what real love from a man is, because she's never felt it. And that's really all she's looking for. As long as she thinks he loves her, she's going to go with what he's telling her. I know it doesn't make it right in any way, and I know you would have to keep your guard up and protect yourself when dealing with her, but you should at least give her a chance ... And I know I've said it a million times baby, but from the bottom of my heart, I feel guilty that the three of you had to go through that ... I understand yawl pain. That's why I empathize with your sister and try to support her through whatever she's going through ... Briana always said, and now I see, you were always the strong one and that's why you became the most successful, even without the illegal crap."

As much as I hated to, I went ahead and told Aunt Sheena what we had been involved with and Briana's blackmail. When shit hit the fan, and after learning of my sisters' betrayal, I had to confide in someone. My aunt seemed like the perfect person to do so with. As terrible as it may seem, my explanation for my role was that, I had tried to take something negative and make it positive. I bought a few rental homes, made stock and bond investments, and now I was financially stable. I expected everyone to use the opportunity to do the same. It wasn't my fault that Briana didn't. We split everything down the middle. She had no right to envy me and make me accountable for the choices she had made.

As a child I was weak and helpless; in and out of foster homes. I refused to be that way as an adult, and that was simply a choice I had consciously made. Briana had a choice as well, so I wasn't budging on my stance on the matter, nor my cold attitude towards her.

"I understand that Aunt Sheena, but it's hard to empathize with that because she crossed her family. Me out of all people." I paused. "She sent someone to my home to muscle me. Do you know how terrified I was? I even sold my house. And the most jacked up thing out of all this is, Onney is dead. That is the big picture here. She took her *life*. Regardless of the fact of her being depressed, Briana's shenanigans added to it. That along with her job investigating her, sent her over the edge. Did Briana stop after that? No. She kept going on with it. I cried on her shoulders over *our* sister and she didn't care. So, Aunt Sheena, I love you, and I mean no disrespect, but to hell with Briana," I said harshly.

Aunt Sheena sat silently on the phone for a minute, and I didn't hear anything but her breathing. She finally responded. "Nijah just give it some thought. I do want to say that nobody is perfect. I've made some bad choices I'm ashamed of too. I've hurt some loved ones as well. I know what Bra is going through, because I've personally been there. If you don't do it for her, do it for me. Even if it's later in the future," she asked.

"I'll think on it Aunt Sheena," I finally said, insincerely. A lot had happened, and I wasn't exactly sure how to fix it. I wasn't the one who should be trying to fix it.

One thing for sure, I wasn't going to make any promises to anyone.

TWO

THE NEXT DAY I thumbed through, and carefully reviewed a stack of papers I had received from one of the Claims Rep's at Aetna. Things were going great at my job since I had been recently promoted to a Supervisor in the Fraud Department. The irony, right … The position came with a $15,000 raise, and the perk of being able to work from home. Working from my house allowed me to continue work on expanding my property business during prime hours. Of course, I couldn't let it interfere with my work for Aetna, but I was the queen of multi-tasking, so I was winning.

So far, I had four new boarding house properties, with plans to buy two more properties within the next six months. That would bring my total to ten units, and produce income of around $8,000 per month, after expenses such as electric, water, and maintenance. At that rate, I would no longer have to use my savings to grow. I could use income produced from the room rentals to buy a new property every three months. My goal was to have around twenty rooming house properties in three years. I had no doubt in my mind that I could do it, especially since I was making good money at Aetna, lived below my means, and had a nice savings to rely on.

I glanced over at the clock and saw that it was close to twelve, so I decided to take a lunch break and get some fresh air. I had been sitting still since eight, and I needed a good stretch. I grabbed my favorite brown Coach bag, and threw on my lightweight, Polo jacket. I had a taste for crab dip and bruschetta, so I hopped in my Mustang for the ten-minute drive to Brick House Tavern.

After returning with my overpriced crab dip, I plopped down in my faux, leather office chair and swung my feet up onto my steel filing cabinet. Right after getting comfortable, I immediately began digging into my crab dip, while savoring the rich blend of crab meat, cream, and cheeses. While reaching over and grabbing my phone, I noticed I had several missed calls from Rashid, and a text message from my new male friend Niseef. Quickly navigating through my phone, I read the message from Niseef:

"Hey sexy, you got some time for me tonight? Miss you and wanna hang out."

I smiled at the thought of Niseef. I had met him months ago through Briana, before our falling out. We had been at the bookstore, Black and Nobel in North Philly, when he walked in. Briana had spoken to him, saying she knew him. The whole time I stared discreetly in awe. He was a beautiful manly sight. He stood around six feet, and had a medium build, but was toned like he lifted weights. He had a low cut and smelled sweet, yet masculine. He had hood swag that he displayed with smoke black Timberland boots, and Levi jeans that actually fit. His face was an average handsome, but the aura that he generated, was not.

After he caught me staring, he introduced himself and extended his hand for me to shake. When I reached my hand out, he wrapped his hands around mine and brought it up to his lips, placing a slow kiss on it. I blushed and smiled sweetly, while pulling my hand away. I introduced myself as Briana's sister, and he continued to follow us around the store, while we shopped for books. On our way out, he stopped me and asked if he could speak with me for a few minutes, without my sister. Briana knew the game and scurried happily to the car, leaving me and Niseef alone.

During our chat, we exchanged numbers, and I had spoken to him sporadically until recently. After Briana and I became estranged I found myself yearning for companionship. Of course, I still had Rashid, but everyone in my life so far, had let me down, including Rashid. I figured it was time I have some fun and got to know Niseef, so I dug his number up in my phone. I didn't want anything long term, I just wanted his company and some excitement to wake up my dull life. No doubt, somewhere in me still loved Rashid, but I had to remind myself that love wasn't enough to stop him from treating me like crap years ago. I wasn't going to put all my eggs in that basket. Besides, I was focused on my daughter, my business, and my job at Aetna; in that order.

<><><>

Later that evening, I parked my car and stepped out wearing black leggings, a fitted gold top and peep toe, split front booties. I looked very sexy, with my curvy body stretching the fabric. The gold top gave my chocolate skin an exotic glow while the tights looked like they had been painted on. I checked myself in my compact mirror, before applying more lip gloss to my full lips. I confirmed I was cute, and then made my way to the entrance of Houlihan's to meet Niseef for dinner.

The restaurant was in Plymouth Meeting, which was about a thirty-minute drive from my house, depending on the traffic. When I entered, I immediately spotted Niseef waving for me from a small booth in a dimly lit corner. I made my way to him and greeted him with a warm hug.

"Hey doll. How are you?" I grinned, inhaling his signature sweet scent. Damn he was fine. He could definitely get it.

"I'm good baby. Glad you could come out. And happy you didn't stand me up like you did the last couple of times," he reminded me. He motioned for me to take a seat.

I dismissed the comment and sat my jacket down beside me in the booth. Smiling flirtatiously, I leaned forward and responded. "So, what's on the agenda tonight?" I asked, while staring into his handsome face. I was extremely attracted to this man.

"Oh, what you got the whole night out?" he asked, his eyebrows raising up in curiosity.

"Something like that," I replied, pushing my long hair being my shoulder.

Layla was hanging out with her dad since it was Friday night. He had been working at his job for a year now, so when he asked to go on day-shift it was immediately approved since there was an opening. It worked well for everyone, with Rashid being able to spend more time with Layla, even seeing her more during the week. He even had a car now, so I didn't have to be the one taking her back and forth.

He was no longer staying at my home as much, since Rashid, even though a true street dude, was known to be clingy and very jealous.

I had tightened up on allowing him to stay with us as much. Coping with my sister's death had become easier, and I now felt safer since I had moved out of the old house right after my falling out with Briana. I had no idea who she had sent over to my home that dreadful night, and I wasn't going to stick around for them to ever come back.

I ended up renting a modest three-bedroom apartment in a nice gated community in Willow Grove. It took me some time to sell my townhouse, so I wasn't rushing into another mortgage. I was saving a lot of money living in the apartment, and Layla enjoyed the amenities that came with it, like the pool. I personally enjoyed the security. No one was getting through those gates, and visitors had to provide proper identification to get into the community as well.

I looked up at Niseef who was waving his hand in front of my face.

"Earth to Nijah," he said with a grin, while still waving.

I smiled. I had been thinking. "Yeah I'll take a Long Island Iced Tea," I finally replied. I would also need a shot afterward. I was just getting started.

Niseef had been asking me what I wanted to drink. He should've been asking; *how many drinks do you want?* For the past few months I had been drinking almost every night. I usually didn't get drunk, but it was certainly more than I had ever drank before.

The liquor helped me sleep at night, and it helped me think less about the situation with Briana. When I was in work mode I was so sure of myself, so confident and poised; however, when it came to relationships, whether it was Rashid, Briana, or Aunt

Sheena, it had at one point been dysfunctional. All of these people had let me down multiple times at some point in the past. It was scary hoping that it wouldn't happen again, but in my mind I knew it probably would. The alcohol was a temporary getaway from life's stress. It wasn't healthy, but hey, it was, what it was.

For the next half hour, Niseef and I talked and laughed over a table full of mainly appetizers. We had so much chemistry and he was extremely easy to talk to. Several times I had to suppress the dirty thoughts I was having about him.

"So Nijah, could you see yourself with someone like me?" Niseef asked unexpectedly. His eyes were glazed and glistening from the liquor, but he was serious.

"I mean you smart and got yourself together. You seem like you go for a different type of dude." Niseef stared at me waiting for a response. Watching me intently he proceeded to stuff a fried butterfly shrimp in his mouth, while flicking the breading crumbs from his fingers into the napkin.

Finally responding, I said, "Believe it or not, I'm a sucker for a street dude. It's just something about their presence and the aura they give off. I mean with me, as long as a man is extremely masculine and is a good provider, I'm open."

"Really?" he asked, eyebrows going up again. It appeared to be a habit of his when he was curious. He took another gulp of his double shot of vodka and looked to me for a response.

"I mean … when I was younger I was attracted to the guys in the street, but clearly most of them weren't husband material. Now as an adult, I'm still attracted to that kind of dude, but all the street crap must be in the past. So, a matured street guy," I joked, laughing. "Honestly, I grew up around those type of guys, but a square would be fine."

"So what type of work you do?" I asked Niseef, turning the conversation to him. We had talked about me enough. I smeared sour cream on top of my loaded potato skin and took a bite.

"Me, I work as a supervisor at the trash company down South West Philly," he said proudly.

"That's good," I exclaimed, highly surprised. Niseef had the hood written all over him with tattoos up his arms and around his neck. It was always good to see young men try to make something of themselves, even when the jobs seemed menial to the world.

"I'm not even gon lie to you though, I do my thing very quietly. I mean I'm thankful for my job. Very. But things get expensive when you're trying to get away from the neighborhoods you grew up in," he confessed, with a serious look on his face.

I figured there was much more to his story. He drove a nice Benz and he just didn't seem to be on a super straight and narrow path. I didn't know what he meant by "he did his thing." For all I knew, he could be robbing people on the side or dealing dope, but I sure wasn't going to ask. This wasn't a confessional booth, and I wasn't trying to get deep.

"Well I definitely understand. I don't judge anybody on how they get it, cuz believe me, I'm no saint. The most important thing is to make it count for something. If you're going to risk your life and freedom, make it worth it," I said, giving my free two cents.

"Trust me baby. I definitely do," he reassured me.

We ended the night by going to see the new horror movie Annabelle. He wanted to continue the evening, but the liquor had hit me, and I wasn't going to wait around to let it hit me harder. When it did, I wanted to be somewhere familiar.

While dropping me back off to my car I told Niseef I would call him later that week. Additionally, he made me promise to see him for lunch on Friday. He wanted to meet during the week, but he worked twelve-hour shifts Monday through Thursday, and I wasn't going to play myself by staying out super late, so I would be tired and unproductive in the morning. Business always came first.

Ending the night, I gave him a kiss that lasted a little longer than expected. I can't lie, he had a sister hot and ready like a Little Caesar's pizza. However, I did the responsible, safe thing and carried my butt home. Lately the liquor had me feeling extra *bad*.

Before I pulled off, I checked my phone to discover that Rashid had called me again. He had called me twice in the restaurant, but I had ignored him since I knew he didn't want anything. If it was important, he would have surely texted me the issue by now. I dialed him back.

"Hey wassup. You called?" I said, asking the rhetorical question.

"Yeah, just seeing if you were okay. Where you at anyway?" he asked.

"I went out with a friend. And Rashid you don't have to call me five times to see if I'm okay. What's Layla doing?"

"Yeah aight. Who you go with Asia?" he asked disregarding the comment, as well as my question. He was being nosey. He already knew that if I said I was with Asia, it would be a lie and I wasn't going to give him the satisfaction of thinking I had to lie to him.

"No, a friend, you don't know them," I said, dismissing the topic. "What's Layla doing, sleeping?" I asked again.

"Yeah. We played monopoly and then went to get some water ice from Rita's. She fell asleep in the car on the way back. Why don't you stay with us tonight?" Rashid asked, abruptly changing the subject again. He was comical.

"No, I'm tired and I'm about to head home." The alcohol I had consumed was steadily creeping up on me and I already knew that going over to Rashid's would lead to having sex. It always did. Rashid knew exactly what he was doing.

"Why don't you just come over here though? I

stay closer than you, and I can hear your voice slurring from where you've been drinking. You can't be out there drunk driving Nijah. Think of Layla," Rashid said laying it on thick, and forcing me to evaluate my decision to drive all the way home.

Exhaling deeply, I agreed. "Aight, you're right. I'll be there in about fifteen minutes." I started my car up and hopped on Germantown Pike to take the drive down to Rashid's, in the Germantown section of Philadelphia. I was feeling nice anyway, so I didn't mind. I made sure to take my time to avoid being pulled over.

By the time I got to Rashid's building I was incredibly relaxed and on cloud nine.

I parked my car in the quiet parking lot and walked the fifteen feet along the side of the building to his apartment door. Before I could even knock, Rashid opened the door. He must have been looking out the window.

"Wassup?" he asked, with a serious look on his handsome, brown face.

"Hey," I responded quietly, while greeting him with a smile. I kicked off my heels at the door and followed Rashid to the living room. He plopped down on the chocolate brown sectional, picked up the controller to his video game, and proceeded to play Fight Night. I sat on the opposite side of the chair and got comfortable.

"You want something to drink?" Rashid asked, picking up a cup from off the coffee table to take a sip. I hadn't detected he had been drinking on the phone when I spoke to him. Had I noticed the slur I wouldn't had come by. He always did the most when he was drunk.

"No, I'm good." I already knew what Rashid was up to. Every time he started drinking he wanted to have sex and get on some emotional male crap. I didn't mind screwing him, it's just that Rashid wanted more than what I was willing to give at the moment. He was used to the past Nijah who was head over heels for him, not the older Nijah who could separate emotions from good sex. It wasn't my fault; it was him who made me that way.

"Yeah I know, you already on," he said sarcastically, with a weird look on his face. He was at it already; emotional and throwing shade.

"Yeah," I replied, nonchalantly, with a grin, not saying what I really had in mind.

"Where you say you go again?" he asked for the second time, while glancing over at me suspiciously.

"I already told you Rashid. And wassup with the twenty-one questions?" I asked, growing irritated.

"I'm just asking. You play a lot of games Nijah." Rashid stared at me briefly, and then shook his head and turned his focus back to his game.

"Yeah aight Rashid. I didn't come over to argue with you about what I do on my spare time. Cuz frankly, it's my business. You worried about who I'm with and on to be quite honest, worried about who I'm screwing," I said bluntly, with a straight face and no emotion. I cared about Rashid but wasn't going there with him. I had to hide my emotions with him because once he saw it, he would use it as a weakness.

He grew irritated and smacked his teeth in frustration. "One minute you act like you trying to make sumn work with us, and the next minute you running around being secretive," he snapped. He paused the game and lay the controller down to turn and face me.

Screwing up my face in disbelief, I asked, "Cuz we have sex? Cuz we have sex, I gotta be tryin to make something work? Ok … so now it's you that doesn't know how the game works right. Before, you screwed chicks all the time you claimed you didn't care about, so that's dead Rashid," I said bringing up the past.

"I'm not gon argue with you. That's not what I came here for. It's Saturday night, I work over fifty hours a week and the last thing I'm going to do is mess up my night arguing. And you really need to relax on the drinking when you have Layla," I said, hypocritically. Yeah, I had a drink or two when Layla was home, but I wasn't emotional and erratic when I drank.

He shot me a funny look and said, "Aren't you the one to talk. And anyway, she's sleep and I worked all day too, so I'm relaxing," he said with an attitude.

Rolling my eyes, I got up off the chair and went to the fridge to get the drink Rashid had originally offered. I had to drown his idiot butt out, just like I did everything else. He was about to get the silent treatment in his own home. I didn't understand why he wanted to argue about *us* every time he got drunk. At the end of the conversation, he would always get the same response.

His real problem was he couldn't dictate what I did, and who I did it with. He didn't want to hear I was having sex with anyone else, but he was acting like that's what he wanted me to confess to. Sad thing was I wasn't dealing with anyone but him. I knew he loved me at the end of the day, but when you love someone you should do right from the beginning. I wasn't about to play myself again, so I would continue to ignore his child-like tantrums. It was funny how the tables turned.

Still standing in the kitchen, I pulled out the opened bottle of Hennessey, and poured me a shot. I quickly swallowed the foul-tasting Cognac and walked to the back of the apartment to take a quick shower. I wasn't worried about clothes since I would just throw back on what I came in, minus the panties of course.

I showered quickly, and when I came out I peeped into the spare bedroom used as Layla's room. I saw that she was sprawled out wildly, still sleeping. I noticed the room now had pink curtains and that Rashid had put in a little dresser and TV for her. I smiled. He really was trying. Maybe I was wrong about him.

The cognac I had drank settled in nicely to my surprise, since I usually didn't mix my liquors. The high I felt from the nights' alcohol had me incredibly relaxed and nice. I walked back into the living room still damp, and boldly stood in front of Rashid. Dropping the thick, blue towel I was wrapped in, I acted like nothing ever happened, and we weren't just bickering twenty minutes ago. I wasn't into games and this is what he really wanted anyway. Besides, I too wanted it in the worse way. I didn't say a word to Rashid; I just waited.

He ignored me for five seconds and then turned the T.V off, peering up at me with glassy, alcohol infused eyes. Grabbing me by my waist, he pulled my naked body down into his lap and kissed my neck gently, then my forehead. Looking directly into my eyes, he asked, "Nijah ... you know I love you right?" he said as he hugged me.

I didn't bother to respond. I just kissed him and then slowly rose up. I was drunk and horny, and I just wanted him to do what he did best: lick me from head to toe and screw me to sleep. I pushed him back, unbuckled his pants and pulled out his swollen manhood. I skillfully and hungrily took him in my mouth. I blame it on the liquor. Had I been sober he wouldn't be getting treated so well. Lately, I was always on, so he was being spoiled. Maybe, that's why he had been so deep in his feelings. Rashid moaned and squirmed while I sucked, slurped, and licked. When I was done getting him rock hard, he reciprocated, and I came the same way I always did.

The next morning, I rose quickly out of Rashid's

warm bed, leaving silently. I didn't want Layla to wake up with me there. She was getting older and I didn't want to confuse her. Seeing me there, she may think we would be getting back together. If it didn't work, she would be crushed. I had given it some thought, but I just wasn't ready. I did care about Rashid; I just didn't have time to pour everything into him again.

For as long as I could remember, I'd always been everyone's rock: the strong one. I was tired of that. I just wanted to be free; free from disappointment. Rashid has let me down multiple times, and Briana drove a stake through my heart with her betrayal. Onney's death had also taken a toll on me. I didn't want anyone to use my shoulders anymore, especially since the only thing that was keeping them up through the day, was a bottle of vodka at night.

THREE

MONDAY CAME FASTER than expected as usual. The beginning of the week I was usually stuck on the phone and swamped in papers to review, but today I found myself on the phone with my realtor Nate. Nate worked for a real estate company in downtown Philadelphia and was helping me buy properties cheaply throughout the city. He had called me to inform me about some cheap homes in the Strawberry Mansion section of the city. The area was up and coming and wasn't as popular for my typical investment of rooming houses. According to Nate, these properties were more profitable to flip and resell.

Figuring it could be a good opportunity to make some larger, quicker cash, I decided to find out more, so I agreed to stop by Nate's office around eleven.

The ride downtown went by quickly thanks to the absence of rush hour traffic, and the soothing voice of John Legend professing his love to some unknown chick in *All of Me*. When I got to my destination, I stepped out looking like business. My Remi hair was bone straight against the black, Ralph Lauren wrap dress I wore. I kept it simple, only wearing gold studs, and a gold cross I never took off. I looked very polished, yet stylish since I had on my white leather, split, peep toe booties by Gianvito Rossi. The shoes were sick and contrasted beautifully against the black. They'd set me back $700, but that was a secret splurge of mine I wouldn't tell anyone.

When I got my money all the way up, I planned to buy a new Audi Q5 SUV to complete my overall look. I wasn't one of those people who liked to fraud, so for now I would stay in my lane with my Mustang. It was good enough for now, allowing me to still look classy while I conducted business.

I parked my car at the attended lot around the corner from Nate's building, and after getting my ticket from the attendant, I took the two-minute walk to the narrow, congested Chestnut Street. I entered the glass double doors of the building and was immediately greeted by the front desk clerk. After signing the visitor log, I made my way up to the fifth floor. I was always amazed at how much the downtown retail space cost when the buildings were so basic. As I walked into Suite 505, I was greeted again, this time, by a more familiar face.

"Good morning Miss Washington, how are you?" Gina asked, with a warm smile.

"I am fabulous. How've you been?" I asked. Gina the receptionist, was one of my favorite people at CT Realty. She was the stereotypical blonde: blue eyed and bubbly.

"I'm wonderful," she said cheerfully. "Haven't seen you in a while and glad you're back. You can go ahead back. Nate's expecting you," she said. With her headset already on, she quickly punched in Nate's extension to let him know I was headed to his office. He was standing at the door before I made it back.

"Hey Nijah!" Nate said brightly, showing his perfect white teeth. He was a very handsome white man in his forties but didn't look a day over thirty-five. He always dressed nice and was great to do business with since he was very straightforward.

"Hey Nate. How are you?" I asked, returning a smile.

"Great! Ready to get some of that cash in your pocketbook!" he joked, still flashing his mega-watt smile. Like I said, he was very straightforward, yet still charismatic and charming.

"First you have to talk some numbers and show me some pictures," I said, sitting down into the comfortable, royal blue office chair. I was ready to get down to business.

"Of course," he said. He walked around his large, mahogany desk and pulled out some photos and passed them to me.

"So, getting right to it, there's two properties I think you'll be interested in. Both are right in the Strawberry Mansion section of the city. The price is phenomenal, and the area is up and coming — Now they will need some work, but once that's done you could easily double your money by reselling them. I wouldn't room these houses out; they're not large enough and there's not as much of a market for it in this family-oriented area."

I looked through the pictures and saw potential but wasn't impressed. One had a gaping hole in the wall, and the other looked like it would need a whole new kitchen and bathroom.

"What's the price?" I asked, finally looking up from the pictures.

"$14,900 a piece, but I believe I can help you get them both for $20,000. The owners are motivated and right now this is a buyer's market. The best part is if you put $10,000 in each house, you could easily see a return of at least $40,000. Spend forty, get back $80,000 — easy. And of course, I'll help you sell them."

I sat silently for a moment while I contemplated the idea. I had been focusing on renting rooms, so I never thought about flipping homes. To me it was risky, but the price was hard to beat, and it could be extremely profitable if done properly.

I looked up at Nate, who was now seated on the other side of his desk waiting for a response.

"Put in my offer. If I fix these houses up you

better sell them for me Nate," I said seriously. "I don't want to lose forty grand."

Even though I had the money, I wasn't into taking losses. At the end of the day, this was business. I made a mental note to do more research on the area. If it wasn't what he said, I would rescind my offer without batting an eyelash.

"You'll never lose Nijah, because even if I couldn't sell them — which I know I can, and will, you could rent them out. So, you don't lose," he replied confidently.

"So, you want to swing over and take a look at them," he asked. "I can tell you my vision, I can show you some price comps for the area, and we can get started on the paperwork. I'm trying to get this deal done while it's still hot," he laughed, before hopping up from his chair.

"Let's go. I have a few hours," I said, before getting up to follow Nate out the door.

<><><>

A few days had passed since my meeting with Nate and since I was paying cash, the closing process was going by quickly and easily. After seeing the properties and hearing Nate's vision, I felt confident with my decision to buy. I had already begun discussing the rehab process with my contractors and had several meetings scheduled to go over what needed to be done. While we were over in Strawberry

Mansion looking at the house, Nate had also shown me a gigantic Victorian house that could be converted into four units: three two bedrooms, and a one bedroom. The price was jaw dropping, and with some renovation, could bring excellent long-term income. Hell, I could even resell it for a staggering price. I was ready to go ham on investing, but I can't lie, it was wearing me out with my regular workload.

Rubbing my tired eyes, I continued to look over some paperwork I had been emailed. I was playing catch-up from the days before. My job at Aetna was easy and straightforward. I made sure my team was handling fraudulent claims properly. Any they had trouble with, or any that weren't as clear, came to me. I also did the monthly call monitoring, as well as coaching and developing with my team.

Lately there had been a lot more shady claims than normal. Since the fraud identifying process was so intricate, it took a lot of time before we were able to label it as actual fraud. Each fraud claim took several hours of review and usually was a build-up of past fraudulent issues. Unfortunately for me, I had about ten on my desk that weren't clear. It would be a long month at this rate.

"Mommy," Layla called. "What time are we eating?" she asked.

Looking up from my work I glanced at the time. It was after eight. Clearly, I had lost track of time.

"I'm sorry honey," I said to Layla, who was standing by the door. "I lost track of time. It's too late to cook. I'll order something. You choose."

"Okay!" she replied excitedly. I usually cooked meals at home, even if it was a bagged, pre-made, skillet meal. Takeout would certainly be a treat for her.

A half hour later we sat on the sofa eating Chinese food. Layla had requested Kung Pao Chicken, which I had never eaten before. She said she had heard someone in school talking about it and wanted to stray from our normal Beef and Broccoli or General Tso's chicken. It actually was tasty.

"So, Mom, the sleepover is tomorrow night. Were you going to drop me off, or was my dad going to?" she asked, between forkfuls of food. Of course, I had forgotten her daycare was having a sleepover for the older girls at the center, sort of like a girl's night.

"Oh shoot! I forgot about the sleepover," I said, slapping my forehead. I can take you. I don't have anywhere to be."

"Ok. I told my dad too. He sounded a little sad that I wouldn't be spending the night with him like usual. I told him we still had Saturday," she said seriously.

I smiled at her comment. Rashid had been doing an excellent job with Layla. I wish he had the same mentality when we were together, however, I always had to remind myself that we both were incredibly young at that time.

"I'm sure he'll be okay honey. Go ahead and finish up your food, so you can brush your teeth and get to bed. I don't want you tired in the morning."

It was now nine thirty and she had to be up early. I on the other hand, would be up for several more hours working on claims. I was going to text Niseef later and cancel our Friday night date. I just had entirely too much work to do.

<><><>

Thank god it's Friday, I thought, as I looked over to the clock on my desk the following day. Unfortunately, it was only 10 o clock and the day had just begun. I had been productive so far, settling two claims. My goal was to have another one done before lunch. I had a meeting with my contractor at 12:45 pm to give him a deposit on the work he was going to do for me. I had settled quickly on the properties in Strawberry Mansion, and estimated repairs to be done in four to six weeks.

I had my hands full for sure with eight occupied rooming houses, and two renovations underway. I was seriously considering hiring someone to help me out. Passive income wasn't always passive. Luckily for me, none of my tenants that rented rooms from me had any complaint's, and everything at my houses were working fine.

With the way things were going, I was expecting to see an estimated income of $11,000 per month. It was modest income, but it was excellent rental property income. That figure didn't include my two-unit, duplex flip which Nate said he could price aggressively at $60,000 each, which was much more than what I expected. I stood to make at least $50,000 cash off that one flip. That could be more if I kept material costs low. If the process went smooth and the sale was a success, then I was going to add flipping houses to my portfolio as well.

After receiving and making over a dozen phone calls, I was tired of looking at claims and dealing with properties. It was just my luck that by the middle of the day, the damn water heater broke at my unit that Aunt Sheena lived in. I had jinxed myself. How the heck the water heater broke so soon was beyond me. I bought it new from Sears, not even six months ago.

After sitting on the phone with Sears customer service and calling my contractor, I had to rearrange my schedule and run down to North Philly to check out the situation. There was also some water that had leaked from the heater, and if it had caused any damage, Sears and I were going to have a problem. It was going to be a long stressful day dealing with all the madness around me, but this was only *part* of what I wanted. I wanted the big bucks, and everyone knows, that always came with a price.

<><><>

Lying peacefully in my tub, I reached over and grabbed the drink that was sitting on the edge of the tub next to my shoulder. I swirled the round, bowl shaped glass around before I took a gulp of the familiar, to put my body at ease. The pale-yellow liquid had only a drop of orange juice. These days, I was using more and more vodka. The concoction went down my throat smoothly. I continued to soak until I heard my phone vibrating on the floor. I reached over quickly, splashing a little bit of water. I thought it might be Layla, whom I had taken to the daycare at seven for the sleepover. To my surprise, it was Niseef.

"Hello," I said, after pushing the accept button on my iPhone.

"Wassup Nijah?" Niseef asked.

"Nothing much, relaxing in the tub. I had a long day," I said. I didn't go into my business too much with Niseef. You never knew what people would do all in the name of a dollar. I had learned that the hard way.

"Damn. Wish I could join you, or you at least join me. I know you said you had been busy and was tired, but I ain't trying to stress you. We can chill, have a drink, get some food. Something laid back, so you can relax. What you think about that?" he asked.

I won't lie, it sounded good, and the liquor had me feeling great, so I agreed. I told him I would be a couple of hours. I had to get dressed and drive to Northeast Philadelphia and I didn't want to rush while he waited. We made plans to meet at Chickie's and Pete's on Roosevelt Boulevard. There wasn't anything like some good hot wings with a glass of vodka and pineapple.

I ended up getting dressed quicker than I thought. I stood in my full-length mirror and admired my appearance. I had on an all-black jumpsuit with a deep V that came to my waist. My chocolate, C-cup breasts were slightly, but tastefully exposed, while my bone straight blend-in weave, flowed seductively to the top of my round backside. Hands down, I looked good. I piled on some raspberry colored lip-gloss from Lancôme and headed out the door.

Before jumping into my car, I called Layla to make sure she was okay. Of course, she was having fun at the sleepover, painting nails and blabbering with her little girlfriends. After speaking with her, I called Niseef to let him know I was on the way. To my surprise, he wasn't answering. By the time I got in contact with him, I was on the Boulevard.

"Yo!" Niseef yelled into the receiver over the massive amount of background noise.

"Hey. I've been calling you. I'm about to get on the Boulevard, where are you? Sounds like you're in a bar," I said, yelling into the phone like he was, so he could hear me.

"Damn, you said two hours, so I figured I had time to have a couple drinks with some of my friends. But that's cool. You're close to where I am. Swing thru here and we can take my car. You said you was tired anyway. I can drive," he offered.

"I don't know about that Niseef. I'm not trying to leave my car in North Philly." The gesture was nice, but that idea was dead. I wasn't new to this. A crackhead would be digging through my whip within ten minutes.

"Aight, well come through real quick. We can have a drink here and I'll say bye to my mans."

"Aight cool. Where you at?" I asked. I didn't have a problem meeting him really quick since I did come earlier than expected.

"The Eagles Bar," he replied, still extra loud.

Frowning my face up, I pulled the phone away from my ear and stared at it. He had to have bumped his head. He wanted me to come to the center of the hood, on Erie Avenue. Here I was dolled all up, and he wanted me to come right into a den of thirsty niggas and hating broads.

"You gotta be kidding me?" I asked in disbelief. "I'm not trying to come off as bourgeois or nothing, but I came out for you, and you want me to come to the damn Eagle's Bar? I mean, Chickie's and Pete's ain't glamorous but it's down Northeast, not North Philly."

"Chill … I got you. I'm only going to be like ten minutes. Promise. And I'll meet you outside. You know niggas gon be tryin to get at ya sexy ass and I ain't having that," he said.

Smacking my teeth, I agreed and altered my route, eventually ending up on the busy, ghetto block of Germantown and Erie.

<><><>

"Damnnn, what's your name sis? Let me holla at you for a minute ma?" was all I heard walking up Germantown Avenue to the corner of Erie. The two bars that were side by side caused limited parking, and I found myself forced further down the block than expected. Niseef met me about a quarter of the way, and boy was I glad; the dudes were thirsty. They acted like they never saw a decent looking chick before. Of course, the looks and the hate of the hood dust-bunnies started before I could even put my custom made, rhinestone heel in the door. I wasn't worried though. I had class, but I wouldn't hesitate to lay hands on any chick that got out of line. I was from the hood too.

Taking a seat at the crowded bar, I ordered my favorite drink, a Long Island Iced Tea. Luckily Niseef knew the bartender so I didn't have to flag her down. She was a cute, younger girl and had her shiny lips pursed together with an attitude. Despite the attitude I still gave her a tip, even though the only tip I should've given her was don't wear faux, fur eyelashes. They looked ridiculous along with the makeup she had caked on. This was why they hate. Instead of taking time to get their look down perfectly, they emulated the trashy looks they considered trends. I didn't follow the ridiculous trends of Philadelphia.

Niseef continued to talk to his two friends. He called himself introducing me in the crowded bar, but of course that was a fail. One of the guys looked a little familiar, and I take it he felt the same, since he kept glancing at me. He called himself doing it discreetly, but I peeped it. Keeping his word, after ten minutes Niseef was ready and we headed out. As I exited the door my heart suddenly dropped. *Here we go with the bull,* I thought.

FOUR

RASHID WAS TALKING to his friend but stopped mid-sentence when he saw me coming out the Eagle's Bar. I cursed myself for bringing my narrow behind out there when I knew he was born and raised in North Philadelphia. This was his stomping ground, and I was like a dumb deer caught in headlights. At the end of the day I was a big girl, and I could do what I want, but I was playing with fire since I knew Rashid was in his feelings and I continued to mess around with him. It wasn't fair, but that's what it was.

"Yo, what the —?" Rashid immediately snarled, while giving me the "ice grill." He didn't even have to finish his statement. I knew what he was thinking. Of course, he hadn't bother to say hello, instead reacting off emotion. I ain't gonna lie though, he was looking good as hell; unfortunately, the scowl on his face messed that all up.

I wasn't sure what to say; I didn't want to go at it with Rashid in front of that many people.

"Let me holla at you real fast Nijah," he said, not really asking. He waved his hand for me to come with him, and immediately walked off without looking back to see if I was coming. I looked at Niseef, and whispered, "Please let me handle this alone." He seemed hesitant but eventually agreed.

I slowly followed behind Rashid to keep things from escalating. Rashid was an emotional hothead and things could get out of order quick. I knew Niseef was from the hood too, and I didn't want a Mexican standoff. I continued around the corner to talk to Rashid. Exiting Erie avenue, we navigated onto Germantown Avenue to in front of a closed store, so we could talk.

"Yo, what the hell you are doing down here Nijah?" he asked, visibly pissed, but still trying to control the volume of his voice. Anger was written on his face.

"I stopped by for a drink. What's the problem?" I asked casually, unintentionally pushing his buttons more. I had my arms crossed against my body, trying my best to act innocent.

"Stop lying — You stopped by for a drink dressed like that? Tight clothes, breasts popping out, ass on display for all of North Philly?" he asked, getting up in my face. I took a step back, but my back quickly met the wall.

"Yep." That's all I could say as Rashid grew angrier with each word I spoke.

"Oh yeah?" he asked, now nose to nose with me. I could smell the alcohol on his breath and hear the malice in his voice.

"Back up Rashid, I'm not doing this with you," I said, growing annoyed. I knew he wasn't going to do much. I extended my hand out, forcing him to back up some.

"I ain't gotta do nothing. I should knock ya head off out here," he growled. "You were about to leave with Boy? Where was you going Nijah? Ready to run off to suck and screw the next niggga," he accused, looking me up and down with his face turned up. The comment amused me just a little, but nevertheless, it was highly disrespectful.

"First of all, don't worry about me Rashid. We ain't together. If I want to stop by and have a drink with a friend, then that's my business. And furthermore, the theatrics is getting old, and I ain't dealing with you like that no more. Our conversations will be limited to our daughter. I don't have time for this stupid crap with you embarrassing me out in public," I said, with an attitude, before attempting to walk off.

"Naaa. Go home Nijah. You not leaving with him while I'm out here," he said, roughly grabbing my arm, and attempting to drag me to my car.

"Get off me Rashid!" I yelled, while attempting to break free from his iron-clad grip.

144

"Yo stop playing with me, before I beat ya ass out here," he threatened. Rashid wasn't typically violent with me, but tonight I guess he'd had enough of my games. I didn't care though, since he put me through more crap then imaginable.

Forcefully dragging me down the street, I pleaded with Rashid to release my arm. Right before reaching the car, I heard a familiar voice calling me from down the street. It was Niseef.

"Nijah. Baby, you alright?" he asked, while cautiously walking up the street towards me and Rashid. People were watching now, and I was praying Rashid didn't make more of a scene.

Giving me a dirty look before releasing my arm, Rashid quickly whipped around and responded. "She's good. Mind ya business," he said, pulling up his khaki pants and exposing his butter colored Timberland boots.

"She is my business. She here with me," Niseef replied coolly. He had reached us on Germantown Avenue, but didn't get too close. The look on his face was one I hadn't seen before. This face was sinister; he was itching to pop off.

"Well this my child's mother and she taking her ass home," Rashid responded, matching Niseef's ice cold stare.

To end the dispute, I decided to just leave; Rashid wasn't going to make it easy to do much else. "It's cool Niseef. I'm good. I'll hit you later. I'ma just leave." I shook my head in frustration.

Staring at me with intensity he said, "Aight cool. Make sure you call." He shot Rashid a look and then hesitantly walked up the street, back towards Erie Avenue. Quickly turning away from Rashid in disgust, I walked the twenty feet up the street to my car. Of course, he was hot on my trail.

"What you want to carry me to the car Hercules?" I spat, mocking his idiotic and jealous behavior.

"Na I don't wanna carry ya big ass, I just want to make sure you get in ya dirty ass car and carry ya stank ass home," he said trying to be funny.

He could laugh all he wanted but I had just saved him from a potential beat down. He was out in the hood acting all love-struck, when he was by himself. Niseef on the other hand, was down there with four guys and would have chewed Rashid up out there.

"Stank? Yeah okay, but you out here acting like a fool over it." I smacked my teeth in disgust and kept walking

"Yep. Now get outta here," he said without shame, as I plopped down in my seat. Slamming the door, I was done listening to him and his foolishness. Turning the key, the engine roared to life, and I peeled off down the block nearly clipping Rashid with my rearview mirror.

<><><>

An hour later I lay back relaxing on my suede,

European chaise lounge that sat across from my bed. The Grey Goose I had at The Eagle's Bar had set in, and I sat peacefully trying to forget the events from earlier. Although I was slightly inebriated by the time I arrived home, I was sober enough to see that Rashid had followed me home. Of course, his stupid behind couldn't get through the gate, so I wasn't worried about him bringing the drama. He had embarrassed me beyond belief. He had been drinking, and that's the only reason I could fathom he would act the way he did. Bringing a bottle of water to my lips to hydrate my dry throat, I heard my buzzer ring. It was security from the gate calling up. They usually called for one thing; permission for a visitor to come in. *I know Rashid ain't coming over here to start some bull, He can miss me with that. He ain't coming up in here,* I thought.

"Helloooo," I said, speaking into the receiver that was right by the front door.

"Good evening, Ms. Washington. I'm sorry to disturb you, but you have a visitor by the name of Niseef Brown. Should we let him up," the Caucasian sounding security guard asked.

Niseef? I wondered what he was doing at my complex and how he knew where I lived. I guess Rashid wasn't the only one that was following me.

"Ummm, yeah sure, let him up," I reluctantly replied. Had Layla been home he would have been sent on his way. I made a mental note to check him about coming to my home unannounced, and about following a me like a stalker. I was already dealing with one idiot; I didn't have time for another. I ran to the bathroom and quickly brushed some lip gloss on my full lips.

I had just grabbed my bottle of Jadore perfume and sprayed the top and bottom of my body before I heard the knock at my door. Taking my time, I walked through my apartment and finally opened the door to see Niseef's handsome face.

"Hey," he said, hesitantly. He had made a bold move by showing up to my house, and his face displayed his nervousness.

"Wassup," I asked with a light smile. I was still standing in the doorway.

"Can I come in?" he asked hesitantly.

"Yea, but I'm going to be going to bed soon. Wassup?" I asked, while reluctantly opening the door and allowing him entrance into my home.

"I came by to check on you. Dude was pretty heated. Just wanted to make sure you were straight," he confessed.

"Well that's nice of you Niseef. I appreciate you checking on me, but I don't usually have much company, and it's kind of creepy you followed me," I said. I wasn't trying to be ignorant since I liked Niseef, but I didn't want anyone following me.

"Well, I'm sorry baby. I just wanted to make sure you were straight. I shoulda called. So that's your baby father?" he asked, casually dismissing his stalkerish behavior.

"Yeah," I said with a smirk.

"Don't look like ol'boy over you. Or maybe I missed something," he said probing for more information.

Rolling my eyes for the tenth time tonight, I responded, "That's a whole notha issue by itself."

"I got time," he said. I guess I did owe him a little bit of an explanation since it must've been extremely uncomfortable for him.

"Well ... first, I apologize for that. I didn't mean to put you, or potentially put you, in any type of situation. My daughter's father is a tad bit jealous. He wants us to be a family, but he did a lot of stuff in the past that prevents that. We still love each other, but I ain't trying to go there with him. Guess he's not understanding that."

"Soooo basically, you're still sleeping with him, he in his feelings, and you still trying to do you," he said, raising that infamous eyebrow. I guess he was trying to make sense of the situation and sum it up in layman's terms.

"That's an inappropriate analysis especially since you aren't my man," I said.

"I could be," he replied. "But the shit that went down earlier, I ain't having. You gotta make sure you and ya child's father have an understanding."

"Well ... me and you aren't at that stages so you're thinking too far in advance. Besides, I know how to handle my business," I said. As soon as I said that, I regretted my slick choice of words.

"Oh yeah?" he asked, boldly moving toward me.

I guess his nervousness had gone out the window. I backed into the door since we were still standing in the foyer talking.

"Handle it then," he said. He was now right in front of me, staring me down.

Pressing his body against mine, I was now pinned up against the front door. My breathing grew heavy once I felt the bulge in his pants pressing against my thigh. Niseef leaned in and kissed my neck. His breathing was raspy.

"Damn you're sexy ... Do you know what I want to do to you?" he asked, whispering into my ear. "I just want to taste it."

I turned my head and shuddered. His words had me weak. How the hell could I resist him? Those lips were perfect. He was perfect.

I led him to my bedroom and seductively sat back on my chaise lounge. I undid the satin robe I had on so Niseef could see my thick, naked body. I seductively spread my legs to reveal my neatly shaven jewels. Licking my lips at Niseef, I invited him to play. After all, he did say he wanted to taste.

Niseef wasted no time coming out of his Timberlands, jeans, and t-shirt. He stood in front of me looking like he was sent from the Heaven's — that was until he came out of his boxers ... When I say Niseef was about a solid five inches, FIRM, I was telling no lie. I didn't say a word. I figured what he lacked in length, he made up for with skill ... I was wrong.

Niseef was awful. He oral was good but that just wasn't enough in my book. I wanted to curse him out when he was on top of me huffing and moaning, throwing weak strokes.

Me being me, I hopped on top to do me, but that backfired. He wasn't prepared for me bouncing up and down on him. He lasted a few minutes' tops. The look on my face confirmed to him I wasn't pleased. I didn't even try to hide it.

To save face, he licked my pearl until I shuddered to make up for his weak performance. He looked good and had lots of swag, but as shallow as it sounds, what I had just encountered was most definitely a deal breaker.

FIVE

"I HAD SOOO much fun mommy. We did our nails and put colored hair pieces in each other's hair," Layla exclaimed excitedly. She was telling me about her awesome night at the sleepover. She turned to the side and showed me the pink clip-on hair extension snapped in her straight hair. It was actually pretty cute.

I had just picked her up from the daycare and we were headed home. The daycare gave us until 10 am to pick up the girls, since they knew a lot of single parents would use the girl's night out for themselves as well. I told Niseef he had to leave at eight, much to his dismay. He was sprawled out, looking super comfortable, and acting like he didn't want to go. However, he didn't have much of a choice. His performance didn't call for any overnight stays, and he most certainly wasn't entitled to any breakfast.

"Well, I'm glad you had fun babe. They gotta do that again sometime soon," I admitted.

"Yesss they do. I like being around the other girls … So, are you taking me to my dads'?" Layla asked. I was praying she didn't ask me that. I didn't understand why she couldn't just hang out with me? I didn't feel like dealing with Rashid and his mouth. However, I wasn't that type of mother or woman, so I was going to do what was best for my daughter and what I had agreed upon.

"Umm yeah. I can take you to your dad's. I didn't know if you wanted to hang out with me though." I said, pretending to pout.

"Mom, I told you I wanted to go to my dad's. How about this, I give you next Saturday okay," she said, offering the proposal, and touching my arm to make sure I was okay with it. I laughed at my daughter and her display of affection and compromise.

"Okay, deal. I'll text your dad and let him know I'll drop you off." Turning the corner, I changed my course and headed to Rashid's.

<><><>

My head was throbbing from last night, so I reached in my purse and shook out an Aleve from a bottle I had. I had just parked my car and was waiting for Layla to get her things. On my way into the building I saw Rashid's Cadillac parked on the side. For some reason it looked odd, sort of like it was leaning. Rashid was at the door since Layla had called him as we were pulling up. After giving her a quick kiss goodbye, I tried to rush off before Rashid could say a word to me, however that move didn't work at all.

"Yo, let me holla at you really quick Nijah," he said, as I tried to walk off. I turned around with an attitude.

"Wassup? I asked, looking down at my watch to appear as if I had somewhere to be.

"Come in real quick. We can talk in private and not in the halls."

I reluctantly agreed and went in. Rashid closed the door when we got in his room. I sat down on the edge of the bed while he leaned against the wall.

"So, what's up Nijah?" he asked, staring at me.

"What you mean?" I asked, smiling, again faking innocence.

"Wassup with you, wassup with life … us. You and I." I rolled my eyes. I couldn't believe this is what he had called me in her for. "What were you doing with dude … and why are you playing games?" he asked. The look on his face was serious and he looked like he wanted for sure answers this time.

"I'm not playing games; I'm just living my life. And the guy you saw me with, was a friend." I said matching his stare. At the end of the day, I was grown. I could admit to what I was doing, but I wasn't going into extra details. It was none of his business.

"Nijah … you're playing games … Listen I'ma keep it real with you, and I'm not drunk. I haven't drunk anything today — I want us to be a family again," he admitted. "This situation is really getting to me. I want to spend more time with Layla, and I can't really handle seeing you with anyone else. I done cut off the chicks I was dealing with a long time ago. I've been dealing with you, and you only. So why you trying to play me on some get back crap, from years ago. You know that's not what you really want."

What he was saying wasn't far from the truth. In actuality we were sleeping together now on a regular basis. He too had been the only person I was dealing with up until Niseef. Honestly, somewhere in my wildest dream we would get back together and live happily ever after. Unfortunately, I had suppressed those dreams a long time ago when he was in and out of jail and running around with this chick and that chick.

I exhaled deeply before speaking. "Rashid … I gave you so many opportunities to do right by me and Layla. So many. You were in an out of jail while I was struggling with your daughter, and when you were home, you provided, but didn't give us your time because you were too busy laid up with God only knows. Regardless of how different you are now, what makes you feel that you deserve anything else more from me. It was me, who dealt with chicks getting out of line. It was me, who was going back and forth to court, with no car, in the cold, pushing Layla in a stroller. It was me, who cried damn near every week, not you. So, you can miss me with that. Don't try and make me feel bad for carrying you exactly how you used to carry me ... Why do I deal with you? Let me think ... because it's good, and convenient. My tongue now had no filter since I was beyond frustrated, and so was he. He paused before responding.

"Nijah, you gotta remember I was twenty-four years old. I was living a fast life and it was fast girls. You always had my heart. I just made mistakes." As soon as he said that, I immediately frowned up my face. He was beginning to push my buttons.

"Mistakes?" I asked, in disbelief. "If it happens once it's a mistake Rashid. When it happens repeatedly, it's a choice. You always have an excuse."

"So, that's how you feel permanently. Soooo, basically I ain't never gon be shit?" he asked. I didn't respond. I just sat there with the "whatever" look.

Growing frustrated Rashid broke the silence. "So, you think we just gon have sex when you want, and you think you gon run around and deal with other men. Yeah okay. Not happening," he said, looking at me like I had lost my mind. I continued to just stare at him. Of course, he kept talking.

"Nijah I've been home *four* years. That's shows that I've changed right there. I stopped dealing dope, found a decent job, and have tried to be a better father to Layla, but you still piss on me. What more do you want? You found out about Kiana and I cut her off. I was messing with her because you weren't even thinking about giving me no play then. I don't deal with nobody else but *you*. Let me show you that I've changed. I promise I would be a different man," he said sincerely.

I shook my head before looking up at him and responding, "I can't Rashid. I just don't want to disappoint Layla, and I don't want to get screwed over by you again."

"We don't have to say anything to Layla right away," he pleaded. "We can continue the way we've been and work on us in the meantime in between time. We can talk, go places, and hang out. At least try. I promise to give you as long as you need to figure things out … and if things don't work out, at least I tried. I know I won't disappoint you. I can make you happy Nijah. I know I can." Damn, the things he said were so tempting. Indeed, I loved him, and I hated that he was bringing those deep old feelings out of me right now. I was always a sucker for the right words.

"Let me give this some thought Rashid," I said, considering what he said. He was right. I loved Rashid, but I had been hurt by him. He had changed a lot, and I did have to remind myself, that we had been together in our early twenties. Six years had passed. Maybe he had changed.

Satisfied with my answer, Rashid went to say something, but was interrupted by a knock at the front door. I looked at Rashid puzzled since he typically didn't have his homey's come over when Layla was there. What surprised me is that he appeared baffled as well. However, he didn't move to get the door.

"Get the door Rashid," I said, since the knocks were getting louder and increasing in frequency. Someone wanted him to come out. Walking to the door, Rashid sighed as he slowly walked to the doorway. As soon as I came behind him and made my way to the door, I could hear the yelling from behind it.

"Open the door Rashid, I see the trick's car outside!" she yelled as she banged.

I immediately recognized the voice. It was Kiana.

"Are you kidding me?" I asked. "She's outta line. Layla is in here, so you best go outside and handle that. I don't want her hearing or seeing none of that project bullcrap. And then you got the nerve to be talking about us getting back together," I whispered, through clenched teeth.

"Nijah this ain't my fault. She been acting stupid since I cut her off. Just chill. Go back in the room with Layla for like five minutes and I'll handle it." Reluctantly, I agreed, and made my way back to the room to make sure Layla was unaware of the drama that was about to unfold.

<><><>

Five minutes passed, and Rashid hadn't come back in the house. Layla was still watching a movie, so I told her to stay in the room, so I could go peek outside. Walking out of the house, I heard screaming. I wasn't ready for the drama that was taking place.

"So how you just gon say forget us for that hoe?!" Kiana screamed, with her finger jammed in Rashid's face.

"Yo, get outta here with the nonsense. There was never a *us*. Don't worry about me or anyone else I deal with. — Go ahead Kiana!" Rashid yelled, extending his arm to create some distance between them after she aggressively approached him again.

A wicked smile formed on my face since the argument confirmed that he had indeed cut her off to try to be with me. As quickly as the smile came, it left when Kiana saw me standing near the steps and made her way to me. Rashid grabbed her but that didn't stop her from talking trash.

"What the hell you smiling for trick. You won't be smiling when I beat ya ass out here?"

I didn't bother to respond, since Kiana clearly wasn't on my level. After all, she was outside begging a man who clearly wanted me, and not her. She continued to talk trash until she saw that it was useless, and I wasn't going to entertain her.

"Screw both yawl! You keep chasing behind that stank, stuck-up hoe Rashid!" she said as she snatched away from him and walked back to her car. "I'll bet ya ass will be running right back to me. That's why the both of you will be walking today!" she yelled, while hanging halfway out her older model Ford Crown Victoria.

When she made the comment, it rolled over my head, until I glanced over at Rashid's car. The reason it looked odd earlier is because all the tires were flat. Looking over to my car I noticed that my tires were flat as well. Dashing away from the spot I had been watching them from, I went over to my car to confirm that my tires were indeed flat. My eyes verified the damage, and I raced to Kiana's Crown Victoria to smack fire out her silly behind. Not surprisingly, she didn't so much as flinch. Her ghetto butt had come for a fight, and that's exactly what she was about to get.

Coming from behind the car door, Kiana quickly formed a fighter's stance. I on the other hand didn't have time for that stance crap, and swung a hard, right hook. I had no tolerance for drama from rat's like her. As soon as I threw the punch, I grabbed her hair and pulled her head down, so I could pummel her. However, Kiana cleverly used her foot to kick my leg from under me. Ghetto chick's like her were used to having tricks up their sleeves to win fights. I should've known better.

Losing my balance, I fell hard, immediately scraping my back on the ground. I still had Kiana's hair tightly gripped in my fist, but she still was leaning over me punching wildly. Even though she could barely see, her punches were still connecting with my face and body. I weakly punched with my free hand, but she was too strong, so I took my right foot and kicked her with all my might. Kiana flew backwards and that gave me three seconds to get the hell up or get my ass whooped.

Like The Incredible Hulk, she immediately hopped up and charged at me. This time I used her tactic; I threw a punch and tripped her at the same time. She fell to the ground, and I immediately hopped on top of her to sit on her, so she couldn't move. There would be no kicking me off. While she thrashed around wildly and kicked to try to get me off her, I gripped her cheap hair and began punching her hard in the face.

I had hit her about two or three times before Rashid came and grabbed me off her. Luckily, a nosey neighbor had called the police when Kiana and Rashid were arguing. Since the neighbor saw Kiana flatten my tires during the argument, she was arrested for vandalism, and Rashid was forced to file a restraining order against her. He was from the hood, but he wasn't stupid. Chick's like her would end up forcing a man to smack them. When that happened, the first person they want to lock up is the male. The restraining order would prove the fact that she was the aggressor, and that he wanted to avoid contact with her.

After all the drama, we decided that it would be best if Layla came home. Since Layla really didn't know what was going on, I suggested that the two of them spend the rest of their Saturday night at my apartment. There was no reason to ruin Layla's day with her father because of someone else's drama.

After calling AAA and getting the cars towed to repair facilities, we caught a cab back to Willow Grove. I was still angry at Rashid, but hid it, since I wasn't squeaky clean either.

The rest of the day went very well. I got ahead at work by finishing up some claims, and also managed to do my cleaning and laundry. Around five I made dinner which consisted of meatloaf, mashed potatoes, and asparagus. I even threw in some chewy, fudge brownies. The rest of the night was movies, and Layla taking turns snuggling up on me and Rashid.

The time for us was very relaxing; I didn't even drink one sip that night. Layla also seemed incredibly happy and it was something I could see myself doing more, something that I was happy to embrace.

I looked over at Rashid and told myself if he did what he said, then we could make it work. However, before I could give my fifty percent, I had a small situation to take care of. A slight problem called *Niseef*.

Niseef had been calling me almost every hour on the hour. He didn't want anything. He was carrying our friendship like it was a relationship and we were a couple. It was becoming annoying since I had other plans for our little "situation". It also didn't help that every time my phone even so much as chirped, Rashid was giving me looks. I definitely needed to handle things fast and figure out what I wanted to do for sure.

SIX

I HANDED THE two crisp dollar bills to the cashier and quickly accepted my change. Throwing it down into an empty cup holder, I reached back out the window and eagerly took my medium Iced Coffee. I took a long sip and smiled; it was sweet just the way I liked it. The sugary, caffeinated drink was just what I needed to get me through the day.

I had just picked up my car from Mr. Tire's to repair the damage from rat face, Kiana. Two tires had cost me over $400, so I was not in the greatest of moods. Best believe I would be seeing that hoe in small claims court. Call me petty; I didn't care. With my police report in hand, I was taking her broke butt to court, so she could reimburse me for the tires I had to buy.

Once a month on a Monday, I took off work and

conducted a visual inspection of my properties. This was just to make sure that the halls weren't littered with trash, and that everything was in working order. Today was one of those days. Unfortunately for me, the day wasn't going so smoothly. One of my places had trash and broken beer bottles all over the front, while another had a cat running rampant through it.

After picking up disgusting ass trash and swatting the cat with a stick, I was irritated and tired. I made a note to mail out a memo about the trash, and not leaving the doors open to allow strays to get in. I would raise the rent if the trash continued to be an issue, especially since I was the one who had to foot the bill when the city fined me for it.

Pulling up to my favorite restaurant, Vivienne's Kitchen, I hopped out and ran in to get my crab cake sandwich. Lunch had long passed, and I was more than aware, because of the pains and sounds coming from my stomach. I got back in the car and heard the familiar ding of my phone. I had over a dozen messages a piece from Rashid and Niseef from the course of the day. I was growing irritated since I was busy, and it was only 2 pm. I still had to check on the work on my rehab, drive back to Willow Grove to pick up Layla early from her after school program, and meet the babysitter at the house so I could make it to the bank in time to deposit rent money orders I had picked up from my P.O Box.

The rest of the day went according to plan, although it was still very hectic. I made it to the bank just in time and headed to the liquor store afterward; I needed a drink. It was around six o clock and starting to get dark when I sat in the car with my bottle of Absolut. I texted the babysitter to make sure that Layla had eaten and done her homework. Rashid had been texting me about coming by his home, but I had other things to deal with at the moment.

Since the babysitter was there, I planned to meet up with Niseef and let him know I wouldn't be seeing him anymore. I could have taken the cowardly route by changing my number, but there was a strong possibility that may not work since he now knew where I lived. The only thing I could do was be honest and cease the game playing. He was fine, but his sex was lacking, and I certainly didn't see him as husband potential.

Dropping my bottle in the passenger seat, I pulled away from the liquor store and made my way over to see Niseef. I would drink later since I wanted to be sober while dealing with him.

<><><>

"Hey boo," I said to Niseef, while walking through the door of his condo. It was small, but undeniably beautiful, in a small suburban area outside of Philadelphia called Bala Cynwyd.

"Wassup sexy. You want something to drink?" he asked, before giving me a moist, uninvited kiss on the lips and leading the way into the kitchen. Of course, that too was small, but was breathtaking with stainless steel appliances and granite countertops. As I quickly scanned the home, I concluded that Niseef was very neat and liked modern fixtures.

Taking the glass, he gave me, I went into the living room and sat down on his black leather couch. There were no personal pictures, just artwork and an exceptionally large flat-screen television. Joining me in the living room, Niseef took a gulp from his identical cup and stared at me with a smile.

"So wassup with you? What did you want to talk to me about?" he asked. He stared at me intently with slight adoration. I could tell he was clearly smitten with me.

I took a deep breath since it was a little hard for me to cut him off. I liked Niseef, and I knew he was feeling me too. He always wanted to spend time with me and was very persistent even though I always had an excuse.

"Well Niseef, I'ma just be straight up with you. I like you but I'ma have to chill with seeing and talking to you. Me and my daughter's father ..." My voice trailed off when I saw his face change. It now displayed a mixture of irritation and anger.

"You and ya daughter's father gon get back together?" he asked, finishing my sentence.

I nodded my head for confirmation. He just stared at me. "Look Niseef. At the end of the day I do still care about him, and I'm trying to do what I gotta do for my daughter. I don't want to spin you, so

I'm just trying to be honest with you. You're a good person, so we definitely can remain friends."

"Friends?" Niseef asked with a smirk, while pausing. "You on some bull Nijah. One minute you act like you single, and ignoring main man calls and texts; the next minute it's a whole notha story you spitting. You're a game player, but I can dig through the bull. I be seeing you on ya phone all the time when you with me ..." He paused again for emphasis. "So, all of a sudden yawl getting back together but we just had sex last week. I guess you slept with him too right?" He sat back on the leather sofa and stared at me intensely, waiting for a response. I hadn't, but I wasn't going to even answer him. Even if I had, it was none of his business anyway.

I smacked my teeth, since the conversation wasn't going the way I wanted it to. I didn't come to argue, in fact, I hated confrontations and disagreements. I just came to let him know what it was; our budding relationship was over.

"That's irrelevant Niseef, and frankly, I didn't come down here to argue," I responded, offended by what he had just said. Niseef was still staring me directly in my face, so I looked down at my fiddling fingers to avoid eye contact.

Niseef paused for a minute, as if he was in thought and finally responded. "Nijah why you want to mess up something that can be good for both of us?" he asked. "I mean ... you told me yaself, the story about all the cheating, and lying. What makes you think anything is gon change? You never gonna be happy if you don't step outside of that and take a chance. You could have that with me," he assured me.

I didn't respond. He was right in a way … however, he didn't know Rashid, so he would never see the change I had saw.

"Look at me Nijah … matter fact, come here … come here," he said, motioning with his hand for me to come to him. I stood up and walked in front of him. He took my hands and looked me in the eye.

"Nijah give me a chance. I mean … you're gonna make your own decision, but don't shut me out. In my opinion he won't live up to the promises he done put in your ear, and then you gonna be disappointed, wishing you had made a different choice. Just don't shut me out," he pleaded. I paused for minute and felt myself warm up with emotions. Damn … I was always a sucker for the right words. My situation would never change if I didn't get my weak ass together.

"Okay Niseef," I responded. What I said to him went against everything I stood for, as well as my internal voice that said *don't do it*. It was done though; I had agreed.

After a couple of drinks and more sweet words from Niseef, I found myself sprawled out on his queen size bed engaged in forbidden relations. I knew what I was doing was wrong, but Niseef was so sexy and at the moment, it felt so right. Right after, I drifted off to sleep peacefully. However, the peace would be short lived.

SEVEN

I WOKE UP abruptly from the blaring sound of my phone going off. The ring was piercing and had also woken up Niseef, who was slowly stretching his body after being spooned against me for several hours. I reached over to his nightstand and grabbed my phone just as the ringing stopped. I wiped sleep out of my eyes to see who it was. It was Aunt Sheena. It was 11 pm which was still early to a night owl like me. However, it was late for Aunt Sheena who was now working the 5 am opening shift at McDonalds.

I quickly scanned through my messages and saw that she texted me.

It's important. Call me ASAP.

I quickly dialed her number to see what was up.

"Hey Aunt Sheena," I asked, as soon as she picked up the phone.

"Nijah where are you? I need you to meet me at Temple Hospital in the ER." Her voice was shaking.

"What's going on Aunt Sheena?" I asked becoming worried. I pushed myself up and sat up straight in the bed.

"It's Briana ... Someone found her. She overdosed."

My aunt's voice trembled with fear. I lost my breath and felt like I was about to pass out the moment she spoke those words. However, my sick feeling was quickly overcome with panic that forced me to move.

"I'm on my way Aunt Sheena." I hung up the phone and quickly jumped out of the bed to get my clothes on.

"What's the matter?" Niseef asked me. I couldn't respond. My mind was focused on one thing and one thing only: my sister. I grabbed my belongings and hurried out of the house.

There was no traffic on City Avenue coming out of Bala Cynwyd, so I was able to quickly hop on I-76 and take the Broad Street exit to Temple University Hospital.

The drive was like déjà vu all over again. It was the same feeling I felt when I went to Onney's; dread. I prayed this time that my sister would be okay. I don't know what I would do if Briana was dead, so I tried to stay positive. I knew one thing; if she was gone I wouldn't be able to live with myself for shutting her out of my life, regardless of what she had done. Something had to change with us, and it had to change quickly.

<><><>

My heart raced as I threw my car in park in front of the automatic doors that read *EMERGENCY ROOM*. Disregarding the fact that it was a no parking zone, I ran through the doors and was met by my Aunt Sheena, who was standing in the lobby talking to a stern faced, middle-age, white man in a lab coat. As I approached the two of them, I saw his badge and realized he was the doctor. Dr. Vick was his name.

I rushed to my Aunt's side as Dr. Vick spoke. Surprisingly, Rashid was already there. He stood up and came by my side as soon as I walked in. I managed to force a worried smile on my face. I appreciated Rashid being right there for me, but I couldn't help the feeling of guilt that weighed down on me. After all, I had just left from Niseef's house.

"Is she okay?" I asked, looking to the doctor while choking back the sob that was begging to escape. I looked at the doctor, my eyes pleading for confirmation.

Aunt Sheena looked to the doctor and said, "It's okay, that's her sister." The doctor cleared his throat and went on to explain.

"Right now, my team is doing the best they can to keep anymore of the drugs from absorbing into her blood stream. We injected her with Naloxone, which reverses the effects of the Opioid, however, she had a lethal amount of Heroin in her system, her blood pressure had dropped tremendously, and she was almost in a coma when she arrived. She will need to be closely monitored for the next few hours to make sure the Naloxone has eliminated the overdose process. Luckily someone found her when they did. Our goal now is to keep her alive. If we can do that, she will need a lot of support as well as some aggressive drug rehabilitation treatment. Judging by the marks on her body and her health condition, this isn't something that occurred over night. There's been some ongoing drug abuse for her, however, the unidentified man she was with, showed no signs of long-term drug abuse, but he was pronounced dead at the scene." Doctor Vick continued to talk but I heard no sound, all I saw were his lips moving.

After he mentioned that she was with a man, my mind zoned out, I didn't hear anything else he said. I knew it had to be Eric. All I remember was feeling the doctor pat my shoulder gently, and whisper words of encouragement. He then walked off quickly down the long hall. At that moment I became overcome with grief. I felt as if I was going to throw up, so I took a deep breath and forced a dry swallow.

As I buried my face in my hands to sob, I felt Rashid wrap his arms around my body to console me. My cries were muffled against his work-shirt. I shook off the feeling of guilt and focused solely on my grief. I looked over to Aunt Sheena who was now sitting in a waiting chair with her face buried in her hands, weeping.

Tears rolled down my face as I prepared to spend the rest of the night in Temple Hospital's emergency room. Without bothering to close my eyes, I quietly took my head from Rashid's chest and looked off to say a silent prayer to God. I prayed that he gets Briana through this ordeal. She had done some messed up stuff, but it wasn't her time. I wondered how she had gotten hooked on Heroin, but then again, I was too busy being angry, and drowning my pain with alcohol.

Loosening up his embrace, Rashid motioned for me to sit down. As I went to sit, the sound of my name being called from the entrance of the ER caused me to refocus. *Shit*, I thought to myself when I saw who it was. Now was not the time.

<><><>

I looked over to Niseef who was standing in the doorway, and then looked at Rashid apologetically. His face flashed anger but was quickly replaced with a more solemn one. I knew he wouldn't make a scene in the hospital, especially since we were there for an important matter. Walking away from Rashid, I slowly walked over to deal with Niseef. I knew he had followed me, and it was getting on my last nerve.

"You okay?" Niseef asked, looking into my eyes with a serious expression plastered on his handsome face. He used his right hand to wipe at a dry tear on my face.

"I'm okay. They found my sister ... she overdosed. She's on machines right now, but I don't really know how it's going to go," I said, with more tears quickly forming and spilling over my eyelids.

"Damn," was all he could say. "Well you know I'm here for you baby. Any time you want to talk; anytime you want to come by or meet up, I'm here," he offered, rubbing my shoulder. He looked like he wanted to hug me. I knew why he didn't; Rashid was probably staring a hole into my back.

"Thank you," was all I managed to muster up. My mind was still bogged down with "what if" thoughts about Briana.

"Well look, I'm gonna go. I'll text you later. I see your baby-father over there giving me the ice grill. I know I shouldn't be here. Stay strong Nijah ... I'll call you okay," he whispered before he walked out. I stood there for a minute and then turned around to go sit down. Rashid was now seated and staring out the window, while Aunt Sheena was pacing the floor of the cold waiting room. I sat down in the green floral chair beside Rashid. Surprisingly, he took my hand into his. I knew that was just the calm before the storm. I said nothing since the most important matter was Briana.

My mind swirled with thoughts that had me jittery. I called the babysitter to let her know I would be in extremely late. She was scheduled to stay overnight in the guest room anyway, so I was merely checking in with her. Layla was already in bed, since by now it was well after midnight. Eventually the events from the night began to catch up with me, and I found myself heavy with fatigue. I closed my eyes and rested my head on Rashid's shoulder. A couple hours later I was awakened by the sound of Dr. Vick. We all stood up quickly to hear the news.

"She's weak but she's going to be alright. We've stabilized her and she's resting, but you all can go in and see her one at a time. We'll probably keep her a few more days until she gets her strength back, but she will be absolutely fine. She's going to need drug treatment. Does she have health insurance?" he asked.

"No, but that's not an issue. You all can send me the bills and I'll see to it she gets the help she needs. I just need some recommendations," I quickly responded. Money would not be a concern as far as getting Briana the help she desperately needed.

Just because I didn't trust my sister, didn't mean I didn't love her. Maybe this was a sign from God. One thing I was sure about, was that my sister needed support. Her drug addiction was likely the cause of her larcenous behavior. I was praying that we could get her some help and she would go back to being the Briana we all knew and loved.

After signing a bunch of papers and giving the hospital my credit card information, we all went back to peek on Briana. She was still asleep and had an IV hooked up to her arm. Her beauty remained intact, but I could still immediately tell that there was definite drug abuse. She had lost quite a bit of weight on her already petite frame. Her skin appeared dull, and her hair was pulled back in a dry bun. Tears immediately began to reform and cascade down my face. Seeing her in that state was not easy. We didn't stay much longer, since it was clear she needed her rest.

Aunt Sheena and I gave Briana a kiss goodbye and then the three of us headed out. I knew this was nobody's doing but Eric, and as soon as she woke up and was strong, I would find the underlying cause of what was going on in her life.

<><><>

"Why was he at the hospital Nijah?" Rashid asked. I knew he was going to bring up the dreaded discussion: it was only right. Despite him being entitled to ask the question, I was still highly irritated. My sister was in a hospital bed and he insisted on coming to my house instead of his, to question me about another man.

"He was just there for support Rashid," I said, trying to quickly get off the subject. I wasn't ready for a slew of questions, and I wasn't in the right mindset to be trying to make up lies.

"Support? Yeah okay … you're lying Nijah," he accused. "I couldn't reach you all night and he just pop up to the hospital for support … Sounds like you were with him before you got there, and you didn't expect me to be there. Why didn't you call me when you found out? Your Aunt Sheena called me when she couldn't get a hold of you. That's the only reason I knew about Briana. Answer those questions Nijah," he demanded, before pausing and waiting for a response. I didn't know what to say so I decided to tell the truth, sort of.

"Look Rashid. I was with him before, but that was only to tell him I was done with seeing him. I had a long day, I lost track of time, and I had a couple of drinks —"

"You sleep with him?" he asked, cutting me off.

"No," I lied. I avoided eye contact with him, so he couldn't detect the blatant lie I was boldly telling.

"Listen to me Nijah, and hear me when I say this … Don't play games with me. That's not what you want. I didn't come into this situation with the same mindset as before. I'm keeping shit real with you, and I expect you to do the same with me. I don't want to find out you're lying to me and that you hiding something … because if you are …"

He didn't finish. He didn't need to; I got the message loud and clear.

"I understand Rashid," I said, before he walked out. I guess he came over just to tell me that. I didn't really like to see Rashid riled up like that. It was extremely uncomfortable for both of us. My momma always told me, emotions weren't to be played with since everyone didn't always know how to control them.

EIGHT

THE NEXT DAY I woke up early despite being up until the wee hours of the morning. After paying my babysitter Ms. Barbara, I tried to conduct business as best as I could. I had informed my manager at work about my family emergency, and he agreed to work with me to the best of his ability. I would still be doing my paperwork as normal, but my availability would be limited to emails and instant messages.

As I headed down to North Philly to pick up my Aunt Sheena, my phone chirped for the tenth time. Niseef had been texting me non-stop, while Rashid had fell back with communicating for the day. He hadn't even called me with his "hey baby, good morning" routine he'd been doing since we started back seeing each other. He was still mad and frankly, I couldn't blame him.

I didn't bother to even look at the messages since by the end of the day, Niseef was going to be blocked. You see, I was a business woman and I wasn't going to change my number and disrupt my business, so I was going to block his pesky butt. That way, no texts, calls, or voicemails would come through from Niseef. I hated to do that but at the end of the day, I wasn't a hoe and I wasn't going to keep going between two men. I wanted to attempt a relationship with Rashid, and it wasn't possible with Niseef bugging every hour and complicating things. I didn't give a damn how sexy he was.

I wasn't about that life in a sense. I knew it was going to be a mess since my behavior today, contradicted my actions and words from yesterday. What a web I had spun.

I pulled up to my building in North Philly and called Aunt Sheena to let her know I was outside. I was picking her up, so we could go to Temple to see Briana. After two minutes, she walked out wearing a purple sundress with her hair braided into a bun. It was the beginning of fall, but it was still warm enough outside to wear a dress without a jacket. She looked nice.

"Hey Aunt Sheena," I said, forcing a bright smile, despite the circumstances.

"Hey Nijah." For some reason she looked a little worried, like something was on her mind.

"You okay?" I asked.

"I'm fine, but I do need to talk to you about

something," she said, adjusting her body in the seat, and pulling down the seatbelt to secure herself.

"Okay," I said, puzzled.

"Stop by McDonalds please. I wanna get a coffee, and then we can park up and talk."

"Okay."

I nervously drove up a few blocks and quickly found a McDonalds. They were plentiful in North Philly, so it didn't take long at all. After ordering Aunt Sheena's coffee, and a strawberry banana smoothie for myself, I parked in the parking lot, so we could discuss whatever she had in mind.

"Wassup, Aunt Sheena?"

I was a little nervous because I wasn't sure what she had to tell me. Whatever it was, she surely had sprung it on me at the last minute, and it seemed important to her, judging by her hesitation. My heart skipped a little as she began to talk. She took a deep breath and spoke.

"Well, hopefully this isn't too much on you at once, but I wanted to do the right thing since it's been burning a hole in me for quite some time now." I raised my eyebrow in curiosity. She had my full attention.

"The doctor called and said Briana is up and doing a whole lot better today. Days before they found her, I told her exactly what I'm about to tell you … Your mom was very good to me …" she said, pausing. I had no idea where Aunt Sheena was going with this conversation, but I decided to just listen and not interrupt.

"She was a lot like you. She had a good heart. She had big dreams. She took very good care of her kids … I was a lot like Briana." Aunt Sheena paused and smiled wearily. "I was loving, but self-centered. And wooooooo", she said, shaking her head for emphasis, "when I got on drugs, the loving part just left with the rest of me. Your father and your mother were together as teenagers. He was killed when you were still a toddler. Your mother never got over that and struggled with depression. With two children to raise by herself, she fell deeper into darkness. She still worked and took care of you all with our mother's help … Well, eventually, our mother got sick and a year later, she passed. That's when things took a turn for the worse. She got strung out on drugs really bad. She had started using during her depression, but she still was functioning. I never said a word. I never warned her about what crack would do to you. I didn't care. I was jealous of your mother. She was everything I wanted to be. I watched her drug herself away, even after what she had done for me."

"I don't mean to cut you off Aunt Sheena," I interrupted politely with a confused look on my face. "But I'm confused," I stammered. "What had she done for you that has you feeling so guilty now, and why did you say my mother was raising two kids after my dad died. I thought we all had the same father. So, Briana has a different dad?" I asked, rambling question after question to make sense out what she was saying.

"Yes, she does ... she has a different father ... because ... Briana's my child Nijah ... not your mother's ... she's my daughter," she said looking away and out the window. What she just said had my mouth wide open. Anything could have flown in it.

"What? Briana is not my sister?" I asked, stunned.

"No. She's your cousin. Your mother raised her until she passed away."

"Why?" I asked, still confused. I had no inclination that Briana wasn't my real sister, and I was truly blown away by the revelation.

"I was so badly strung out Nijah. When Briana was six months old, I went on a week-long crack binge. I was in and out of the house with a bunch of random men and women. Briana was there alone half the time. Your mother was calling me, and not getting an answer. So, she decided to just pop up at my house to check up on me one day. When she came by, the door was unlocked, and I was passed out with a man in the living room while Briana was in the back room on the floor screaming. She had fallen, and she was hungry. She hadn't eaten, and she was soiled up her back. I saw her, I heard her, but the crack consumed me ... That day, your mother took her. She said as long as Briana had family in this world, she would be loved. And that's what she did. She loved Briana like her own. This was before she got on drugs. When she got on drugs I didn't think about all that she had done for me. I didn't think about you girls. I just thought about how perfect your mom always seemed and how imperfect she really was by being on drugs. I wanted people to see that. They judged me so harshly, but she was always praised. In a sense I was happy. Happy that she finally showed the world she was no better than me." Her voice trailed off.

"Gosh I was so messed up. I was jealous, I was hateful, and I was spiteful. I was just like my child Briana is ... to you."

I didn't say anything, but it made sense. Briana did always look a little different. She was always lighter, and she was a lot smaller than me and Onney. No one would have ever questioned it because my mother had never treated her any different from the rest of us, and I had never even heard so much of a whisper about this family secret.

"Wow," was all I could say. "So, you told Briana this?" I asked, feeling a bit deceived.

"Yes. She was shocked but she too, said it made sense. Listen Nijah, the main thing I want to get at is, Briana isn't well. She's hooked on drugs, and she had a very dysfunctional relationship with Eric. She needs help. She needs rehab and she need therapy, so she can let go of whatever's making her bitter towards you. But here me when I say this, don't let her hatred break you down. I've seen the wear and tear on your spirit since this has happened. You are a wonderful person, but *you* must see that. I noticed that you've been drinking all the time since you two fell out. I noticed you overwork yourself … and I also noticed this new guy that was at the hospital. When I called Rashid last night I expected you to be with him. When that guy popped up at the hospital, I realized then, that you were playing with fire."

"I know Aunt Sheena," I said, looking away. She damn sure didn't miss a beat, and I had done my best to hide my struggle within. "I'm going to take care of that, and I'm gonna also get myself together. I've been feeling guilt when it comes to Briana and I don't understand it. That's why I drink. It helps me cope with everything. I always felt like I did something wrong. Like I failed her somehow. My greed consumed me. Onney lost her life behind my greed … my scheme. I feel like I don't deserve what I have. It's like I want this fairy tale life, and it's in front of me, but I can't accept it, because I don't deserve it. I don't even know what I deserve anymore."

"You can have a good life Nijah, and you *will* have it; you just have to accept it. You can't blame yourself for everything, especially Onney's death. You all were adults. You all made informed choices, and she choose to take her life. She had options, just like you did. You fought under pressure, while she gave up. You can't take the blame for that, and you can't blame yourself for Briana either. You are only responsible for *Nijah*. It took me years to leave that person within me behind. Until she's able to do the same, all you can do is support her with distance, filtering your love. And Rashid loves you too. I hear it in his voice. I see it in his eyes. You just have to let him show you with his heart. People change, and I do believe that he has."

"I know ... I'll make it right," I said tearfully. "Everything ... I love you Aunt Sheena, and I'm glad you're well, and in my life."

"I love you too baby, and so does your sister Briana, deep within her heart. Until she shows it, you focus on the ones around you, that *are* showing it. And you accept it, because you are worthy of it."

<><><>

The conversation with Aunt Sheena brought a lot of clarity to my life and had me feeling like a weight had been lifted off my shoulder. I never really spoke much of my feelings of guilt for Onney's death and Briana's actions. Now thinking about it, I don't know why I would blame myself behind how Briana acted anyway. I guess being her older sibling, *or so I thought*, made me feel like I was responsible for her. No matter what anyone said, I still felt like I failed her.

I found a place to park on a run-down street a few blocks from Temple Hospital after we arrived. I hit my key fob twice to make sure my door was locked, and after stepping around numerous potholes, we arrived at the entrance and made our way up to the fourth floor where Briana was staying. I knew it would be awkward going in there after my aunt's revelation, but I had to talk to Briana, find out what was going on with her, and let her know that I cared.

Walking into the room my emotions were mixed. Bra was sitting on the bed and I didn't know whether to slap her or hug her. I was happy as hell she was alive and well, but I was still angry with her for her betrayal. For now, I wouldn't focus on that. I figured if I could find the underlying cause of what was going on with her, then everything would eventually make sense.

"Hey how are you feeling?" I asked, putting down my purse in the visitor's chair beside the bed.

"I — I'm okay," she stammered, quickly looking at Aunt Sheena and then back at me.

"So, this is your surprise?" Briana asked, still looking at me, but talking to Aunt Sheena. Aunt Sheena nodded.

"Briana has been asking about you and Layla. She didn't expect you to come up here, but I told her that's not your character. You're love for her outweighs all." She turned to Briana to speak.

"She forgives you Briana, but she needs answers. We need to know what's going on with you. What made you do the things you did, and how you ended up in here?" I didn't say a word. I just looked at Briana and waited for a response.

"Where do I begin ..." she huffed, before her eyes began to water. Aunt Sheena went over and rubbed her back, while Briana lowered her head and nervously tugged on her plastic hospital bracelet.

"Ever since we were young, it's been difficult

overcoming the feeling of being unloved ... I mean, I knew you loved me, and Onney sometimes, but I always felt like I was missing something ... I was always jealous of Nijah." She finally looked up at me and began speaking to me directly.

"You were always prettier, had a nicer shape and all the cute guys wanted to talk to you. Hell, I even had a crush on Rashid back in the day before you two got together; back when he used to be on the block," she laughed dryly.

"You were always so strong, so sure of yourself. You had a vision for us, to get us out of poverty and make it. You always got on me about my grades and about the stuff I was doing out in the streets. I knew you loved me, but I couldn't help but envy you. I wanted to be just like you ... When you got out of community college and got the job at Aetna I became even more jealous. When we started getting big money I tried to step my game up ... but it wasn't enough. Here you were, buying properties, getting promoted at Aetna, and about to open a nail salon. I wasn't doing anything comparable. I felt like I could never please you. The money was serious. I wanted to party. I wanted to have fun. I started getting high ... smoking weed. And just as quickly as the money came, it went. I envied you," she repeated. "I wanted your life ... and then, I met Eric ... He treated me so good in the beginning. He had me thinking I was his everything, his number one." Her voice cracked at the mere mention of Eric. I knew it must have been hard talking about him since he had passed.

"I opened up a little too much. I let him know how much money we were getting. He started asking questions. He played me against you. He talked about how selfish you were, and how you were stacking your money and getting rich while I was messing mine up. It was all a game to him ..." Her voice trailed off as she stared out the window.

"One day when I was drunk, he introduced me to a new drug. He said he did it all the time, but he never said what it was. I found out later that it was Heroin. By then it was too late ... and like that, I was broke." She snapped her finger for emphasis. "Well, I was damn near broke anyway. That's when he introduced the idea of blackmailing you. I hated myself ... but the drugs took over. It was a struggle just keeping myself up, so you wouldn't notice. Over time the signs started showing, and eventually you found out. That was just the beginning of my problems. Even though I did what I did, you still gave me my half of the money. I thought Eric would be happy. He wasn't though. He was furious. He said I was careless ... that you never should have discovered our identity. He wanted more. That joint bank account was the worst idea of my life. He took damn near every bit of that money. One day while he was taking a shower, someone called his phone. It was a woman. His wife ... Eric was married." Briana paused and choked back a sob. I too was tearing up. My sister had been brainwashed and used.

"She and I started arguing on the phone. I lied and told her I was pregnant. That's when the truth came out. She started screaming on the phone about how Eric didn't care about me and that she knew about me the whole time … That he was taking my money and bringing it home to her *and* their two kids. He had just deposited $35,000 in *their* account. The worst part was Eric never used heroin. He sold it. He had intentionally gotten me hooked on it to use me. Here I was … trying to fit in with him like a fool … destroying myself … and my family." Briana cried and shook her head from side to side, before placing them in her hands."

"I felt so betrayed," she continued. "I loved him so much. You were right," she said, looking up at me with a tear stained face. "I hated him, and I hated myself … so while he was sleep, I loaded up the syringe with a strong cut, and poisoned him with the same thing he was poisoning me with. I ended him the same way he had ended me … I wanted him dead, and I wanted to be dead too. Cops really didn't care … they didn't even ask what happened. They just saw two black junkies who had overdosed. One dead and one barely clinging to life," she said, with emptiness.

The room was silent for a couple of minutes while we let all that Briana had said sink in. *Wow* was all I could think.

I got up and went over to the bed to give her a hug. I empathized with all that she had been through, and my heart ached for her, however, the focus now was to get her well. After a couple minutes of saying nothing, I proceeded.

"Listen Briana," I said, finally speaking for the first time since I had gotten in the room. "I forgive you, but I will never forget what you did. I love you and that's why I'm standing here today. If you cross me again, I will write you off for good ... You need help, and we want to get it for you. I've already called Valley Forge Treatment Center and they can take you in as early as tomorrow. It's a thirty-day inpatient treatment, and it's in Norristown. I figured it would be easy if you were in a different environment. I know thirty days seems like a long time, but your body will need time to get used to being off Heroin. After that, I will pay for all three of us to go to therapy. Clearly, we have some trust and resentment issues we need to work on. If this is okay with you, then I'll go ahead and set everything up. If it's not, then I won't ... But I do want to be clear that this is the *only* way that we can move forward. This is the only way that we can work on having any type of relationship ever again," I said sincerely. The ultimatum had been given. I waited patiently for her to respond.

"Okay," she said. "I want us to be a family again," she replied, quietly.

So, it was settled. I arranged to pick Briana up the next day in the afternoon when she was discharged. I was praying that rehab would be enough to get her on the right track. I knew it would be a long road and this was only the beginning.

NINE

ON THE RIDE home I felt a sense of calm. I would finally be getting my baby sister back. Sister, cousin, whatever you wanted to call it. She was still my sister to me. With things on track and arranged for Briana, I decided it was time to refocus my energy solely on my home.

Layla had been seeing Ms. Barbara more than her own mother, and Rashid and I were barely speaking. I was ready to make things right and bring peace to my life. I had already blocked Niseef since he continued to call non-stop like a deranged person. I was starting to think that Niseef wasn't wrapped too tight. He showed such weird behavior. He was clingy, obsessive, and very persistent, which was a sharp contrast from the self-assured and confident attitude he initially displayed.

I peeked at the clock on my stereo and realized it was lunch time, so I figured I'd catch Rashid while he was on his lunch break at work.

While still focused on the road, I reached into my oversized purse to grab my phone. After voice dialing Rashid, I waited for him to answer.

"Hello," he answered in a distorted voice. He sounded like he had a mouthful of food.

"Hey Rashid. How are you?" I asked, hoping he was in a better mood today.

"I'm good. How'd everything go at the hospital today? I know you said you were going back up there," he said, while chomping and swallowing on the last of whatever he was eating.

"Everything went well. Briana agreed to go to a drug treatment program I found, so I'll be taking her over there tomorrow to get her admitted ... So much has happened today. I'll tell you all about it later. I was hoping you were coming by tonight. I'm going to make some lasagna and spend some time with Layla. It's gonna be quiet for the most part."

"Yeah, I'll be by after I get off. I need you to wash my uniform for me though. I ain't gon feel like driving all the way home tonight and getting up that early to do it."

"I gotchu boo," I said before saying bye and hanging up the phone. I was so happy he was in a better mood. Rashid was one of those people that didn't dwell on things. He addressed it, and that was that.

Before driving off, I returned a few emails from my phone, and afterwards, began my journey back to Willow Grove. First, I had to stop to the market and get the ingredients for tonight's dinner.

<><><>

Rashid walked in around six in the evening. There had been an accident on the expressway, so he was a little later than I had predicted. As usual, he was tired, so I told him to go relax and I would have dinner ready soon.

After piling on a final generous layer of cheeses, I shoved the pan of lasagna in the oven. My five-cheese lasagna was the bomb, and I couldn't wait to dig into it. I peeked in the living room at Layla and Rashid, only to see that they were curled up watching the Disney show, I could certainly get used to seeing that every day. They looked so beautiful together, and it wasn't anything like coming home to a house filled with love.

Rashid had truly grown up. He wasn't out running the streets anymore, he was working, and he was saving his money. He wanted *us* to work out. The ball was in my court, and I was going to make it work.

An hour and a half later, everyone had eaten, and fatigue was setting in. I sent Layla to bathe, and I began loading up the dishes in the dishwasher.

"Rashid, you know where everything is, so you can go and get ready for bed if you want. I know you gotta be up early to get to work on time. You have some boxers here from before. I'll wash your uniform for you. Just leave it out," I yelled into the living room, while simultaneously scraping food away from the plate I was holding.

"Aight, cool. Where you want me to sleep?" he asked.

"Where else?" I replied, with a mischievous grin.

Smiling back, he replied, "I can get used to this for sure."

TEN

I PULLED ONTO the side block of the hospital I had grown accustomed to parking on during Briana's short stay at Temple. Before getting out, I checked my emails, and made a mental note to reply later.

I had just dropped Layla off at school, and I was still a little tired from the night before. Rubbing my eyes, I stared into the mirror, and confirmed that I still looked presentable, despite how I felt. I slathered another coat of clear lip-gloss on my plump lips and got out of the car to walk up to the hospital.

Today was the big day. Briana was being released around noon, and I was going to take her to lunch before driving her over to Norristown to the rehab facility. I was excited. It had been months since our falling out, and I was eager to move on from all the negativity and drama.

Walking up to the hospital, I was oblivious to the fact that someone was walking up behind me, until I heard my name being called.

"Nijah hold up," a familiar voice called to me. As I went to turn around I felt a strong hand grab my arm. Pulling away, I spun around and saw Niseef.

"Uhh, hey. Wassup," I said hesitantly. I took a deep breath. He didn't look very friendly, so I wanted to limit the conversation.

"Wassup with you *stranger*?" he said with emphasis. "You ignoring me, acting all brand new," he said. I was no longer walking, instead, I was standing on the curb not too far from the hospital.

"Look Niseef, I have a lot going on right now. I'm just focused on getting things right with me and —"

"You and who? Ya baby father," he asked, cutting me off. I smacked my teeth and turned around to walk away. I didn't have time for the nonsense.

"Bitch, I'm talking to you, where you going?" he asked, while grabbing my arm again to stop me. I turned around and looked at him like he had lost his mind. The man before me, I didn't recognize. He had done a complete 360.

"Bitch?" I asked, to make sure he hadn't lost his mind. "Niseef don't disrespect me, and definitely don't play yourself. I blocked you because you bug. I have entirely too much going on to accommodate that nonsense. For the record, you and I don't exist.

Maybe in another world ... Don't get me wrong, you're good people, just not right for me. But please, don't come out her and discredit yourself by acting like less of a man."

"So, you back with that clown now. How though? We just talked about this," he said while inching closer to me. The muscles in his jaws. He was truly bugging out, and I wanted no parts of it.

"Look Niseef, for the last time, I'm good. I'm going to try to make things work with my baby father. I apologize for leading you on. We can remain friends, but I can't deal with you like that anymore," I said sincerely.

He shook his head in disgust. "You foul as shit. You trying to shit on me. I can get any chick out here," he boasted.

"Well go get em Niseef. If that's the case, then why you standing here?" I asked. Before I knew it, he had grabbed me by the collar of my jacket and pulled me into him.

"You wanna be cute? I'll make ya fuckin life hell," he said, with a snarl.

I snatched away, and yelled, "Don't ever put ya hands on me again, you nut," I yelled, with wide eyes.

"Bitch you haven't seen a nut. But you will." He walked off and didn't look back. I stood there staring at his back, as he proceeded down the street, and turned the corner.

I had heard the stories, but never had I dealt with a fatal attraction type of situation. I mean, I had experienced the jealousy … but this, this was something different. Niseef wasn't wrapped too tight. I could see the look in his eyes. He clearly wasn't taking rejection well. I cursed myself, since this was all my fault. I would tell people what they wanted to hear and then rescind, like they were crazy. The lies and games were catching up to me, and I didn't like it one bit.

I shrugged off the bad vibes I had developed and continued the walk up and into the hospital. I continued up to the fourth floor to Briana's room, where I was greeted with a warm smile.

She looked a lot better sitting on the edge of the bed. She was still thin, but she seemed a lot better in spirit than before.

"Hey Nijah," she said, standing up to give me a hug.

"Hey sweetie," I said, while embracing her. "I see you're ready. Did they give you release papers yet?" I asked. Briana had her little hospital bag neatly packed and placed by the door. Aunt Sheena had brought her something to wear, so she looked nice and put together.

"No not yet. They told me they would have them ready in about an hour." She sat back down on the bed.

"Let me ask you something Briana … Do you remember the guy Niseef that I met at the book store, Black and Nobel? We were in there together, and you introduced me, saying he was a friend."

"Oh yeah, I remember that day. Niseef is a friend of Eric's brother.

As soon as Briana spoke those words, my stomach churned. Anyone affiliated with Eric was probably bad news. Eric was a scumbag potential killer, and I knew the apple didn't fall too far from the tree.

"Oh, I didn't know that," I said nonchalantly.

"Niseef never came around much," she continued. "I met him a few times. He was on a different level. He was only a couple years older than Eric, but he had a different vibe about him. He was always quiet, but everyone always seemed to flock to him. He was always with Rodney, Eric's older brother. Remember when Onney died, Rodney was in the car with Eric when he drove us up to her house."

As soon as she said that, a bell went off in my head. I remembered Rodney! I only glanced at him a couple of times in the car during the ride, but he was with Niseef the night at the Eagles Bar. That's why he kept staring. He remembered me, but I didn't recognize him. It seemed odd that he didn't speak.

"Oh ok, I remember Rodney now," I said, not going into too much detail with Briana.

"Why you ask about Niseef?" Briana asked, curiously.

"No reason. I had gone out for drinks with him a few times," I lied.

"Oh well be careful girl. That's if you plan to see him again. I heard that he was in the disposal business."

"Disposal business? What the hell is that?" I asked naively.

"Eric told me that Niseef is kind of like the hood hit man. ... He puts anyone to sleep for the right amount of money. Supposedly he's good at it too. I heard he has a nice ass condo out in the county, along with plenty money tucked in the bank off them bodies."

"Oh wow," I said. Truthfully, that was all I could even get out. I was at a loss for words. Niseef was a contract killer and I had just put him in the worst place to be: his feelings. I didn't understand how someone that could murder so easily, find rejection so hard to deal with.

I decided to get off the topic of Niseef. Lately I wasn't having the best of luck. I contemplated getting a restraining order. He had already shown me that he could easily follow and find me. He knew where I lived, and he flat out said he would make my life hell. I was once again terrified, waiting for someone else to decide how my life would play out.

After waiting about two hours, the nurse finally showed up with Briana's release papers. She had only been there for three days, but it seemed longer. After thanking the staff, we said bye and headed to Maggiano's downtown. I figured I would feed her good before she went to the rehab. Lord knows what they would have on their menu, and besides, kicking heroin was no easy task so I wanted to treat her before she began the grueling process.

In the hospital, Briana was given medication to take away the cravings for the drug, but outside it was a whole different story. She was already getting a little fidgety and was scratching at her arm periodically.

We walked into Maggiano's Little Italy right before the lunch rush, so luckily, we didn't have to wait for a table. The host sat us at a small, two-person booth, in a quiet corner of the restaurant. Two minutes later, our server, a brown-haired young man, by the name of Tom, brought us water and proceeded to take our order.

I ordered Shrimp Scampi, while Briana got the Shrimp Fra Diavolo. I glanced at the time and saw it was 11:15 am. I was right on time to have her over in Norristown and checked in before 3. My goal was to get her there early and get back well before it was time to pick up Layla from her after school program.

We made small talk for twenty minutes until our food arrived. I wasted no time digging into the plate of piping hot scampi. While I ate, my phone began to vibrate repeatedly. I looked down and didn't recognize the number, so I didn't answer it. The vibration stopped and within ten seconds, it began again.

"Why you don't answer that?" Briana asked, while shoving a forkful of shrimp, and fettuccini in her mouth.

"I don't recognize the number," I said.

Briana laughed and asked, "What you got bill

collectors calling or something? Not Big Money Nijah," she said sarcastically. The comment was said like it was supposed to be a joke, but I didn't miss a beat. I remembered what Aunt Sheena said, and dismissed it as pure jealousy. I paid all my bills in full and on time. She knew damn well it wasn't a bill collector.

I grabbed my phone off the wooden booth and decided to answer the unknown number.

"Hello," I said, hesitantly.

"Hey baby," Niseef said, greeting me. He was clearly being ridiculous, like I hadn't just told him to "go to hell" just a couple of hours ago. Without responding, I immediately hung up the phone.

"Can't stand telemarketers," I lied, so Briana wouldn't ask me any questions.

We finished our food a half hour later and made our way to Norristown. After getting Briana settled in, I prepared for my journey back home. I had the next day off, and I would use that to relax since I would be going back to my regular work schedule the upcoming Monday.

I looked down at my phone for the hundredth time that afternoon. The messages I had received sent chills through my body.

I'll destroy you and that little family of yours. Try me.

I didn't need to ask, I already knew. What I didn't understand was how a grown man was acting so immature just because a female didn't want him. I shook my head, still baffled by the whole ordeal. My

Aunt Sheena told me I was playing with fire. I wonder if she knew anything else about Niseef. I was surely going to ask her.

I was going to wait to tell Rashid about what Niseef was up to. I loved Rashid, but I didn't want him trying to step to Niseef. I didn't want to get him caught up in the drama. There was no telling what Niseef might do.

ELEVEN

It was around nine the next morning when I walked out of the Criminal Justice Center on Filbert Street, fuming.

I had gone in to get a restraining order but was dismissed. I was told that I didn't have a justifiable reason to have a restraining order issued. According to them, "I'll make your life hell," wasn't technically a threat. The multiple times he followed me also didn't quite classify as stalking, especially since we had only recently stopped being intimate. They wanted him to follow me a few more times after we stopped being intimate, and then it would be considered stalking. All I could do was roll my eyes and take deep breaths to keep from going off.

No wonder chicks were getting killed left and right by deranged lovers. I was at a crossroad. Niseef was still calling. Each time he called from a different number. I was starting to think he really didn't even have a job like he said. He had way much time on his hands.

Just as I was crossing the street to head to my car, my phone rang. This time the number came up as unknown.

"Hellooo?" I asked frustrated. The phone games were getting annoying.

"Nijah — don't hang up," Niseef said, quickly.

"What do you want Niseef? I told you it's over between us. This is getting annoying and it's not cute at all."

"I know Nijah … and I don't know why you got me acting like this. I can't help how I feel about you. You lied to me and I'm just upset," he explained.

"Well, I'm sorry … I really do apologize. What I did was wrong but please, leave me alone," I begged. I looked around cautiously before climbing into the seat of my Mustang. There was no telling where he was at.

"Bitch, it's not over, till I say it's over," he snapped, in a threatening tone.

Pausing into the phone, I responded. "Niseef, I just filed a restraining order against you. This is stalking. Your sex is whack and so are you!" I yelled so he could give it a rest. I don't know why I assumed insulting him would help the situation.

"You think I care about a damn restraining order," he spat, cutting me off in midsentence. None of the other stuff I had just said to him registered.

"Niseef, you are above this, just leave me alone please," I whined. I rubbed my temple in frustration.

"No Nijah ... I'm above you. And I will be above you, when I stomp out all your teeth," he threatened. The words he spoke came out cold with venom.

I quickly hung up the phone. I wanted to cry. He said he would make my life hell and that's exactly what he was doing. I was at a crossroads. I had to wait for a restraining order, and Niseef wasn't backing off. I was scared. My plan was to limit my movement for a little while, until he stopped bothering me. There was nothing else I could do, and my hands were tied.

<><><>

Two weeks passed, and things were going well. Briana was doing very well in rehab and was two weeks from coming home. She was getting back to her old, shallow self again.

The first week had been hell for her because of the heroin withdrawals. She would scream, kick, curse, cry, throw up, and anything else you could imagine from a heroin addict in withdrawal. Watching her in that state was hard, but Aunt Sheena and I did it.

I walked through the fancy, secured gates of Valley Forge Treatment Center, and waited to be buzzed in. After showing my id to the security guard and signing in, I walked back to the outside lunch area where Briana was eating at a small table, by the swimming pool

"Hey boo," I said, greeting Briana, who was eating a BLT.

"Hey Nijah," she said with a smile, before wiping her hands on a napkin and pushing her sandwich to the side.

"Just came to see how you were doing and talk to you a little bit about something. How's everything going?" I asked while having a seat.

"It's going good. Ready to get out of here and get back to my house. I know I have a ton of mail."

"Actually, Aunt Sheena has been stopping by to put your mail up and make sure the neighbor's dog hasn't been pooping in the yard," I laughed. "You know they got into it right. The dog had pooped all up in your yard and Aunt Sheena stepped in some,

I laughed thinking about what had happened. "You already know she was heated, so she walked over there and told them to keep the dog out the yard. The lady called herself getting smart, and Aunt Sheena told her she would whoop her ass and smear the dog poop in her face when she was done."

Briana was in tears as I told her the story.

"Naaa, but on a more serious note," I said, as I wiped the laughter tears out of my eyes. "I wanted to talk to you about something serious."

"Wassup?" Bri asked, curiously.

"Well, Rashid got promoted to training supervisor at the meat processing plant he works at. His actual training for the job begins in two weeks and lasts for a month."

"That's wassup girl. Rashid doing his thing. Yawl back together?" she asked smiling.

"Yeah. It's going well. We had been seeing each other on and off months, and then we decided that we were going to make it work. For the past few weeks he been at my place though," my voice trailed off. "The job is in Baltimore Briana," I said quickly, with a serious look.

"He asked for us to come with him … Layla and I … so we can start over and be a family. He wants me to wrap up what I have going on here and we get a condo together out in Baltimore. By the time he's finished his training we will already be settled in." I waited for her to respond.

When Rashid proposed the idea, I didn't hesitate. So much had happened in Philly, and it was time to get away. I had plenty money in the bank, a wonderful job, and more recently a beautiful, complete family. It also didn't hurt that I would be able to free myself from Niseef's crazy, stupid butt.

Lately, he had fell back with the phone calls, but I still didn't feel safe. I figured moving would be a fresh start.

After waiting a few seconds, Briana finally responded. "I think that would be good for you Nijah," she said with a smile. "I'm genuinely happy for you. Did you tell Layla yet?" she asked.

"No. She's going to be excited about moving to another place, but she's not going to want to leave her friends and school. I think she'll be ok though. I don't plan to put her in private school in Maryland. We're going to get a nice condo out in the suburbs and she'll go to a good school out there. Really, I'll be able to save more money."

"What are you going to do about your properties and job?"

"I'm going to keep them. And, I was thinking about letting a property management company handle them. They'll charge me like 30%, but they will handle collecting rent and dealing with maintenance issue. As far as my job, I work from home now. I'll probably have to drive back a few times a month for meetings but, that's not a problem."

"Well you got it figured out Nijah. I think you'll do great. Make the move boo," she said, seemingly sincere.

"Thanks, Bri. So, I was thinking that maybe ... you and Aunt Sheena should come too ... move out of Philly. You could find a job in Baltimore, and I'm sure Aunt Sheena could work at another McDonalds out there or find something else."

"Girl, I don't know about that. I love Philly. I wanna do hair, and this is the place to be," she said, before taking another bite out of her BLT.

"Well just think about it, ok," I asked.

"I will." Briana looked down at her watch and

hopped up. "Oh shoot. My therapy session is in ten minutes. I have to go to that. Thanks for coming Nijah. Let me know how everything goes with the house-hunt." She smiled and leaned over to give me a hug.

"I will. And I'll be by in a couple of days to check on you."

"Okay. And thanks again Nijah ... for everything."

"Of course, sis," I said, with a smile, before getting up from the table and leaving.

I really appreciated the gratitude. I just wanted her to know that no matter what we went through, I had her back and I wanted to help her. I was more so happy that she was willing to accept it.

The rehab had set me back $5,000, so I was happy Briana seemed to be getting better. In my eyes, it was worth every penny.

I left Norristown with the intention of stopping downtown to see Nate. My rehabbed properties were about finished, and I wanted to put them on the market as soon as possible. The whole rehab process had been progressing quite smoothly, but I wanted to sell quickly since I would be moving soon.

My goal was to have a place in a month, so by the time Rashid came, everything would be situated. I was going to try to make the move as simple as possible for everyone, including myself. I had so much to do in four weeks, but I was ready.

<>‹><>

The trip to see Nate went better than I had expected. After taking a quick drive to my partially rehabbed properties in Strawberry Mansion, Nate intended to list them both at $39,999. I was cool with the price since I skimped and saved while buying materials. I spent way less money than Nate had suggested, so it was only fair that I got back less than he had initially projected for the sale of the two houses.

I didn't care, I just wanted to unload them and make my money back. Nate already had a potential buyer; a couple who were looking to buy some rental properties. I was excited. This was a new beginning for me, and like Aunt Sheena said, I deserved it.

After leaving Nate, I made a pit stop to North Philly to see Aunt Sheena, since it was her day off. Her birthday was coming up in a few weeks, so I wanted to pick her brain, so I could buy her the perfect gift. I figured I would take her to a late lunch. Nobody loved food more than I, so of course I always wanted to invite people to sit, eat and talk.

I pulled in front of the house and sent Aunt Sheena a text to let her know I was out front. As I waited I noticed a black Ford Crown Victoria riding slowly up the block. It didn't stop, but something seemed fishy. Since the neighborhood wasn't the best, I dismissed it, and texted, *hurry up.*

I wasn't trying to get caught up in any hood beefs. This was another reason I wanted my aunt to move when I did. I bought the house for income, but I had no plans or desire to live in it, especially considering it was North Philly. It was a good idea for Aunt Sheena temporarily, but we had to see about getting her out the area.

After another minute, Aunt Sheena came out with a big smile on her face. She had her usual bun in her head but was rocking regular blue jeans and a plain black t-shirt. I smiled back at my Aunt but frowned when I saw the Crown Vic pull back on the block. Just as Aunt Sheena came down the steps and started walking to my car, shots rang out.

I screamed as my aunt hit the ground, while the Crown Vic barreled down the street at full speed. Fear paralyzed me, but once the car turned the block and was gone, reality set in, and I realized I had to help my aunt.

I struggled to get out of the car as adrenaline and panic gripped my body. Blood poured from my Aunt Sheena's arm as she struggled to get up. She had been hit. I screamed internally as I grabbed her and quickly helped her into the car. I ran around to get in the driver's seat, so I could get her to the hospital.

"Oh my god! Oh my god!" I cried. "Put pressure on it. Don't let it bleed out," I told Aunt Sheena, so her wound wouldn't leak out as much. I mashed down on the accelerator and headed to Temple Hospital.

"Ahh, it hurts!" she yelled, in pain.

"It's okay Aunt Sheena, I'm gonna get you some

help," I cried.

Since the hospital wasn't far, I got there in less than five minutes.

I parked directly in front of the emergency room, and the feeling of déjà vu overcame me. After yanking the passenger door open, I helped my aunt get out of the car, while I yelled for help. People in the waiting room looked at me like I had lost my mind. She had been shot in the arm, so I guess they figured it wasn't that serious. I didn't care though. I didn't live like that, and to me, gun-shot wounds were not the norm.

A couple of nurses ran over to assist, while telling me to stand back. Before I knew it, Aunt Sheena had been whisked away in a wheel chair, and I was standing there in the ER still in tears. I turned around to go back and move my car, but my vibrating phone in my pocket stopped me. The number was blocked. I knew it was Niseef.

I didn't even bother to answer. I already knew what type of time he was on. I knew he was off, but I underestimated him. I knew Niseef was behind the shooting and I was terrified. He knew where I lived, and he had found the rental house with no problems. I had told him I owned property, but I never showed him where they were. Just while I was thinking about Niseef being involved, I got a text message from a random, unknown number. It read, *tell auntie to be safe*, along with a smiley face emoji.

I shook my head silently. There was no telling what else he would do, or what else he knew. I thought about Layla and Rashid. Tears streamed down my face. I was screwed. I had gotten Aunt Sheena shot, and I had no choice but to go and tell Rashid about the mess I had created. This time it was no one else's mess that had gotten me in trouble. I had spun my own web. Things were way out of hand, and I no longer knew if I would be able to fix them.

TWELVE

IT WAS MIDNIGHT, and I sat on the sofa, waiting for Rashid to respond. He was ticked beyond comprehension.

"Nijah why the hell hadn't you been told me what was going on?" he asked, jaws clenching.

"I was scared. I thought I could handle him —"

"No. You didn't want me to find out you were still seeing him!" he yelled, staring at me with disgust.

"Yeah ... that too," I said in a low tone.

He shook his head and stood up from the chair. "So, what you tell the cops?" he asked.

Rashid wanted vengeance, but I wanted to let the cops handle it. I knew it wasn't a lot they could do since we didn't see the face of whoever was in the car. I gave them as much information about Niseef as I could, so they could at least question him and lock him up for something — anything.

"I told them what I knew, how I met him, as well as how he's been following me." I paused before saying the rest. "I told them where he lives, and the anonymous phone call and text message I got right after taking Aunt Sheena to the hospital." I looked over at Rashid, who was still giving me the look of death.

"Right now, they said all they can do is question him, and finally give me the restraining order I requested before." He looked up and glanced over at me.

"How long this been going on Nijah?" he asked.

I sighed. "I met Niseef before you and I got back together ... before we even started seeing each other again."

"But you never ended it when I asked you to, right?" he asked.

"I tried Rashid ... I really tried. He wouldn't take no for answer. Once I became firm, he got hostile and started acting crazy. He popped up on me at the hospital and we exchanged words. After that, he just did a complete three-sixty."

"Where dude be at?" he asked angrily.

"Why Rashid ... I already told you what time he be on. I don't want you getting into something you're not ready for." I regretted putting it in those terms. Rashid looked at me with a bruised ego.

"I can handle whatever, and I'm about whatever," he growled angrily.

Trying to save face, I said, "I know Rashid, but let the cops handle it. That way no one will get in trouble over this … ok?" I assured him.

"Alright Nijah. Either way, we out … You get on top of the house hunt as soon as possible … And I just want to be clear. I'm with you, no matter what. I'm not scared of anyone, but I fear what I might have to do to protect my family."

"Thanks Rashid. And I'll get on that house hunt," I said with a smile, ignoring his last comment. "I'ma go check on Aunt Sheena ok?"

I got up and walked to my bedroom where Aunt Sheena was sleep, recovering from the gunshot wound to her arm. Right after she was discharged from the hospital, I brought her to my home. There was no way I was letting her step foot back into the apartment. I would gather her things with Rashid later. In the meantime, we were all together.

I peeked out the blinds to see if the police officer was still stationed outside of the building. Whenever a crime against a person occurred, it was procedure for a cop to sit outside for a day or two for added safety.

As expected, the cop was still stationed in front of the building quietly. I left the room and went into Layla's room to give her a kiss. She too was sleeping peacefully. I didn't plan to send her to school in the morning, or anymore mornings for that matter. I was going to withdraw her and send her back to school in a few weeks when we left for Maryland. I'd rather be safe than sorry. God knows I wouldn't be able to live with myself if something happened to my baby.

I decided I would call Briana in the morning, however, Aunt Sheena made me promise to not tell her what was going on. She felt that is was for the better. With her treatment still in progress, it was best to keep her focused on getting better.

A little while later, I went into the guestroom of my house and climbed into the full-size bed. Luckily, I had kept it as a guest room, instead of just using it for my office. I wanted Aunt Sheena to be comfortable, so I let her have my room; plus, I had to get back to work in the morning.

I pulled the covers up high to my chin and scooted close to Rashid, wrapping my arm around him. Surprisingly, he was still awake. Reaching over, he gently put his hand over my arm.

He didn't have to say anything: his touch told it all. I knew the only reason Rashid was putting up with my drama, was because he had put me through so much in our past relationship. I wasn't trying to go tick for tack, and I appreciated everything he was doing.

After a few minutes of staring at the soft black waves in the back of Rashid's head, sleep overcame me.

<><><>

Two weeks had passed, and I was uber excited. Briana had been released from the rehab and was back to her old self. I had found a beautiful condo in a quiet suburb outside of Baltimore, called Glen Burnie. The movers were loading up the last of my things, while I stood in the now empty apartment talking to Briana and my Aunt Sheena.

"I am going to miss you both. Six months is too long," I pouted.

"We're gonna miss you too, but I gotta wait until the new store opens to leave," Aunt Sheena replied, proudly. She had been offered an opportunity to train as an assistant store manager for a brand-new store in Baltimore City.

She had asked if she could transfer to be closer to us, but they gave her something even better; a new job offer along with a promotion, because of her stellar performance. I planned to sweeten the pot right before she moved by buying her a nice, used car. I had my eye on a newer model Toyota Corolla. Something nice, and reliable but that wouldn't break the bank. I was extremely proud of her and I wanted to show her. She deserved it, since she literally took a bullet for me.

Thankfully, Niseef had been caught on an unrelated shooting. Once he went under investigation for Aunt Sheena's shooting, the police spotted him at a bar and were finally able to pull him over for a routine traffic stop. Because of the strong odor of marijuana smoke, they were able to search his car and found a gun that was linked to an earlier shooting. I guess everyone gets caught slipping at some point.

I hated to find joy in someone else's pain, but I was happy they caught him. I was going to flee Philly undetected, and move on with my life. The sad part was, I had genuinely liked Niseef, but he was the true definition of a cold nutcase. Turning my attention back to Aunt Sheena, I wrapped my arms around her and gave her a big hug.

"I'm proud of you Aunt Sheena … and I love you so much," I gushed.

"Thank you, baby," she replied. "And I love you too." Releasing her, I switched my focus to Briana. I wrapped my arms around her in a warm embrace.

"I'm proud of you too Briana. This has been a long hard year for you, but you kicked through it. You've been through a lot and you proved your strength." I released her and wiped a tear from my eye. They were about to leave, and soon I was too. Layla and I were going to be getting on the road in an hour and head to our new home. It was bitter sweet, but I knew it was best.

I had to pat myself on the back, because in two short weeks I had found us a home, sold two investment properties, and found a property management company to manage my remaining properties. Things were going well, and the last thing I needed to do was transfer some money from my old bank to a smaller, local bank in Maryland.

After watching the movers load up the remaining items and head to Maryland, I slowly got in my car with Layla to head to the bank before we began the drive. I looked back at the apartment building and sighed. I would miss this place.

<><><>

It was amazing how one negative event could nearly ruin your day. Walking out of the Bank of America, I took a few deep breaths to keep from flipping out. I had gone there to withdraw a considerable sum of money, but they told me they could only give me $5,000 in cash. I didn't understand how I had several hundred thousand dollars in that bank, but they could only manage to scrape up $5,000 to give me. Talking about they were low on bills. That wasn't my problem.

After causing a ruckus, which got me nowhere, I took my money and left. I made a mental note to cancel the account completely and take my business elsewhere. Had it been an emergency I would have been out of luck.

I texted Rashid and let him know we were in route to the new house and he immediately texted back a smiley face. He would be joining us in a month and I couldn't wait. Layla was especially happy when we told her, mommy and daddy would be giving it another shot. Our family was complete and there was nothing that could stop us.

THIRTEEN

3 months later

"I DON'T KNOW Aunt Sheena. At the last minute, she called and said she wasn't coming. She said she would be on the first train this morning. I called her earlier and she didn't answer. She hasn't been answering all day," I said, worried.

Three months had passed since we had gotten settled in our new condo, and I had invited Aunt Sheena and Briana to visit. Aunt Sheena came as planned, but Briana was a no show, and now she also wasn't answering the phone.

"I don't know what's going on, but I'm worried. Everything seemed fine with her. She seemed normal. She was working down at the Weave Bar washing hair, and she was supposed to start hair school in a month." She shook her head before saying, "I'm going back tomorrow. I want to make sure everything is okay with her."

"No Aunt Sheena. I'm sure she's fine. If we don't hear from her, then we can both drive over to Philly."

"You can't be doing all that traveling Nijah. You're five months pregnant," Rashid butted in from across the room.

"I know Rashid, but I gotta check on Briana."

"Briana's a big girl. I'm sure she's fine, but you gotta make sure you chill on the running around and unneeded stress," he added.

As much as I hated to admit, he was right. Shortly after arriving in Maryland, I discovered I was eight weeks pregnant. The bouts of tiredness were finally explained. After the initial shock, Rashid and I sat down, and I confirmed that it was his child since he was the only person I had been with unprotected. Since then, Rashid and Layla were super excited, and I can't lie, I was too.

"Well I can take the train back. I can't rest knowing that something could be wrong," Aunt Sheena said. I could see the worry on her face. We both were worried.

"Okay Aunt Sheena. If that makes you rest better, then I'll buy and print the ticket first thing in the morning … but I'm sure she's fine."

"I just have a funny feeling Nijah." I prayed she was wrong.

<><><>

The next morning finally came and we still hadn't heard a word from Briana. As promised, I bought Aunt Sheena a ticket, so she could go back to Philly to check on her. She had two weeks off, so she would return in a few days.

With swollen feet, I walked to the night stand to get my keys, so I could run Aunt Sheena down to the train station. Before my hand could grip them up, I heard a knock at the door. It was probably Briana, all late and wrong. Maybe her phone had died, or she had gotten lost. I told her I would pick her up from the train station when we planned the visit, but she insisted she catch a cab since I was pregnant.

I didn't bother to look out the peephole and quickly snatched the door open. My heart sank when I didn't see my sister at the door. Instead, I saw two white men in crisp suits, as well as a uniformed police officer.

"Hi. Are you Nijah Washington?" the older of the two men asked. He had gray hair and had on a gray suit that made him appear washed out.

"That's me … and you are?" I asked, becoming a bit nervous as Aunt Sheena walked up behind me. I hoped nothing was wrong with Briana.

"I'm Officer Richard Franklin with the United States Government, and we're here to issue an arrest warrant for you. You are under arrest for tax fraud, and evasion."

"Oh my God," I said, as my throat immediately dried up and my head started spinning. I looked at Aunt Sheena, and told her to call Rashid, who had already left for work.

Turning me around, the uniformed officer grabbed my wrists and placed cold metal cuffs over them. I knew when I walked out of the door that it would be a while before I stepped foot back through them. I was glad Rashid and Layla weren't there, so they didn't have to see me like this, but I was also sad because I wouldn't be able to kiss them goodbye.

<><><>

A year later, after pleading guilty to tax fraud and tax evasion, I was sentenced to two years' house arrest, as well as twelve months in a federal correctional facility. The legal fees to get that sentence nearly crippled Rashid and I.

Through the turmoil I managed to give birth to a beautiful, healthy baby boy named Isaiah. He was the main reason I was able to get two years' house arrest instead of doing it in a federal penitentiary. Once the two years were up, I would turn myself in and begin a year-long prison sentence. All my rental properties were seized, my bank account was frozen, and I was neutralized down to nothing.

It turned out that Briana had been running her mouth to a so-called friend, and once they had a falling out, her friend blabbed to the IRS. My so-called sister in turn, ratted me out to take the heat off herself. It was funny since I thought that if we ever went down for the tax fraud, it would be because of Onney's role and the internal investigation they had over there. Of course, they brought that up to help their case. In the end, Briana walked away with a year-long sentence because she labeled me the master-mind behind the scheme.

I ended up losing my job since there was no way I would be able to continue holding a position in the fraud department since I now had a federal fraud conviction. They ended up giving my position to my dear friend Asia, who had stuck with me even when I had been labeled a "greedy monster" who took advantage of vulnerable inmates. She even came to my defense by standing up for me as a character witness. For those reasons, I loved her dearly and would forever be grateful for her.

Despite all the adversity, I still wasn't bitter. I had a beautiful family, a husband that loved me, and a wonderful Aunt. She had even moved in during my legal woes to help with expenses. Aunt Sheena had even finally gotten the courage to wash her hands of Briana, saying, "until she saw the light, she would walk alone in darkness."

One day my sister and I would eventually cross paths again, and I would smile. You see, I wasn't stupid by a long shot. I knew there was always a possibility that this could happen, especially after the blackmailing incident. After taking my properties and seizing my cash out of my accounts, I had managed to pay off a good amount of what the Feds said I owed. What I did still owe, I made payment arrangements over five years to pay off the remaining balance.

Despite all the madness I had been through, once everything was over, my family and I would take a nice vacation to the Cayman Islands ... That was where I had a safely tucked, fed-free, offshore account that would keep all the drama I'd been through, from being in vain.

FOLLOW UPTOWN BOOKS ON INSTAGRAM

http://www.instagram.com/uptownbooks_publishing

If you enjoyed this title by Shontaiye, check out **Messiah Raye**, also under Uptown Books.

https://www.amazon.com/-/e/B01L3N8SWE

Questions/Comments/Add to Mailing List

Email us at

uptownbookspublication@yahoo.com

If you enjoy reading, please leave a review.

FOLLOW ME ON SOCIAL MEDIA
instagram.com/shontaiye
twitter.com/LaRekaShontaiye
amazon.com/author/shontaiye
www.goodreads.com/Shontaiye

CPSIA information can be obtained
at www.ICGtesting.com
Printed in the USA
LVHW011926101218
599940LV00002B/232

9 781728 853383